DECLAN REEDE: THE UNTOLD STORY
(BOOK 0.5)

MICHELLE IRWIN

COPYRIGHT

DEDICATION

To the Aussies who want their "u"s back in the language.
To the people overseas who want to learn more about the flavour
and colour of life in the land of Oz (and don't mind the word fuck).

To the closet revheads and racing wannabes.
To the ones who remember their first love, their first regrets, and
the moment life became "real."

This book is for you all.

To my stunning cover models who agreed to be the embodiment of
my characters.

I couldn't have done it without Jenny who helped give me the push
to do something I thought I never would; without my family beside
my side; without the secret inspirations for this story who will
forever remain nameless; and without my support network firmly
in place around me.

And finally to Gabby who was the first to ignite the spark of desire
to write about the sexy V8 driver who has grown up to become
Declan Reede.

CONTENTS

GLOSSARY:

Note: This book is set in Australia, as such it uses Australian \ UK spelling and some Australian slang. Although you should be able to understand the novella without a glossary, there is always fun to be had in learning new words.

Bench: Counter.

Boxing Day: The day after Christmas. It's a public (bank) holiday and different families have different traditions for it.

Esky: Cooler (ice-box).

Formal: Prom.

Having kittens: Panicking or feeling stressed.

High School Certificate: High school diploma.

Kit (sport): Outfit. To "kit up" is to get dressed in your sporting outfit.

Newsagency: A shop which sells newspapers/magazines/lotto tickets. Similar to a convenience store, but without the food.

Oval (school): Field. It's where all the sporting events happen, usually whole school parades, it's more often than not used for general play at lunch, and as an evacuation point for fire drills.

Ranga: Ginger/redhead.

Sick Bay: School nurse (note: most Aussie schools don't have a nurse, just a teacher who will call your parents).

Schoolies: Week-long (or more) celebration for year twelves graduating school. Similar to spring break. The Gold Coast is a popular destination for school leavers from all around the country, and they usually have a number of organised events, including alcohol-free events as a percentage of school leavers are usually under eighteen (the legal drinking age in Australia).

Scrag: Whore/slut.

Tunnel Ball: A game played in almost all primary schools where students line up and pass a ball down the 'tunnel' formed by their legs. The end of the tunnel picks the ball up and runs to the front of the group while everyone else shuffles back and they pass the ball through the tunnel again. Continues until the original leader is at the front. Played as a competition sport on sports day (school sporting carnival).

Wag: Ditch school.

Uni: University.

PROLOGUE

"What we call the beginning is often the end.
And to make an end is to make a beginning.
The end is where we start from."
~ T.S. Eliot ~

AT THE AGE of nine, life was easy.

Boys and girls were able to be friends, *just* friends, with no ulterior motives and no pesky hormones getting in the way. That's the way things were between me and my best friend, Alyssa Dawson. Simple. Easy. Whether we were at her house on a Sunday afternoon playing monopoly with her brother, Josh, watching a movie, or swimming at the local pool, it was all effortless.

Life itself was something measured in the moments of fun between the drudgery of school lessons and helping with chores. Marriage, kids, the future, they were all foreign concepts not needing any consideration on a day-to-day basis. A career was something parents had and didn't require any thought outside of creating an endless list of "when I grow ups." My own list was a little less endless than most. It only ever consisted of one item. One goal: I would be a V8 driver, or I would die trying.

At some point after nine, things changed. There was no discernible moment when it happened, it just did. One day things were uncomplicated, the next, they were different. Girls were no longer just people to befriend on the playground. They were interesting in a way that boys never were—at least not for me. Girls became mystifying and bizarre.

At that point, it seemed like boys and girls couldn't be *just* friends anymore.

That's how it was with Alyssa and me. She was still my best

friend, but something had shifted. When we entered high school, I noticed things about her that I'd never seen before, and it wasn't just the obvious physical changes like her boobs and hips. A hundred smaller things grabbed my attention, without me even realising I'd seen them.

Little things, like the way her lips would caress the end of a pencil as she studied. The way her fingers would twine loosely in her chestnut hair when she was deep in thought. The way her mouth would curl up in a secretive smile when she daydreamed. Her cute pout when something didn't go her way and the fire that flashed in her eyes when someone pissed her off.

It wasn't just Alyssa either.

By the time I was fifteen, it was like all girls were a different species that both fascinated and frightened me. They all gave me the feeling of snakes writhing in my belly. Hand-quivering, pit-of-my-stomach dread when I needed to talk to them alone. They all made me yearn for things that I didn't really understand—newly-awakened desires that filled my nights with fantasies. Emotions I could no longer control roiled and duelled within me.

More than anything, I wanted to experience the soft caress of lips like the ones Alyssa wrapped around her pencils. Have gentle fingers stoke my hair or trail along my skin.

About the same time I first noticed those things, life in general changed.

In no time at all, things became complicated. Our focus was no longer board games, TV, and summer fun, but study, university, careers, and, well, life in the broader sense. The future was no longer a distant objective we could worry about at a later date. It was real and it was happening. We each needed to make a plan for the future and work hard to earn it. In order to steer our lives in the right direction, we had to make choices.

I had to make choices.

My vision for what I wanted had always been so clear, but suddenly I was paralysed with fear.

What if I chose wrong?

CHAPTER ONE

THE END OF FRIENDSHIP

OUR KISS WAS soft and slow.

It was warm and welcoming.

Alyssa tasted absolutely divine as our lips dragged across one another's in a perfect melding. The scent of the crushed grass around us provided the backdrop to our surprise first kiss in the hot December sun. I knew if I opened my eyes, I would see the unbelievable image of her body pinned beneath me while I kissed her until we were both breathless. No doubt her hair would be fanned out behind her, rich deep brown against the green ground. I didn't want to open my eyes though, because it would only ruin the moment.

She hummed against me as one of my hands found its way to the base of her neck, twisting gently into her hair. She cupped my face before fisting her fingers into my hair and tugged slightly, pulling me closer to her. I opened my mouth in response, granting her tongue access to explore. Every swirl of her tongue or shift of her fingers was done in a way that I was certain was designed to drive me mad. Each touch drew a new sound from me, one I'd never made before, or had even known I could make.

The kiss was passionate and fuelled by desire. It was unlike anything I'd ever experienced before. In the instant it had started, I knew I'd never really kissed anyone before. Not properly. Not like this. I'd wanted to. Just three days earlier, I'd been half mad with desire for Darcy Kinsley. I'd been obsessed in the way only a fifteen-year-old boy could be. I'd imagined having my tongue in her mouth and her boobs in my palms.

All thoughts of her had been completely obliterated by one kiss.

The fact that I was sharing it with Alyssa was more than I could have ever imagined.

She'd been my best friend for years, but maybe not anymore.

I pulled away a fraction and met her honey-gold eyes. Her breath brushed across my mouth, and my tongue trailed forward to slick my lips in response. My gaze refused to move from hers despite the call of her lips. A quiver ran through my body and my heart pounded against my ribs. My voice held almost no volume, was just a breathless whisper as I uttered the only word running through my head. "Wow."

"Yeah," she breathed back.

Closing my eyes, I tipped forward and touched my lips to hers again. The instant we reconnected, a throaty groan escaped from her and she opened her lips for me once more. The action made my stomach clench and sent chain reactions echoing down my body. I was so completely lost in her—in us—that I didn't hear anyone approaching. "Declan? Alyssa!"

I jolted at the sound of my name. Alyssa chuckled against my lips. The feel of her shifting beneath me sent a surge of whatever new emotion I was feeling through me. My heart clenched, my stomach fluttered, and my lips burned with the need to touch hers again. Unable to resist, I renewed my attack on her mouth.

"Seriously?" A tone of disgust rang in Josh's voice.

Although I was tempted to ignore Alyssa's older brother and just keep kissing her, she seemed less than comfortable with continuing our PDA in front of him. She placed her hands on my shoulders and gently pushed me away. Despite the movement, a dreamy smile lit her face and I could see she had no regrets—even after being caught in the act.

After pulling myself up into a seated position, I offered my hand to help her up too. We sat cross-legged, facing each other. My hands played with her long locks, twisting the dark ends around my fingers as I studied her gaze, looking for any signs of what might happen next. I refused to relinquish my hold on her completely though, or break the moment so soon, because I wasn't sure I'd get the chance to do it ever again.

"What the hell are you two doing?" Josh asked.

I risked a quick glance at him, and then around the park we were in. Scattered around us was half a deck of cards. The other half had been blown across the park by the wind while we'd been otherwise occupied.

Totally worth it, I thought to myself as Alyssa's tongue stroked her lip before she offered me a small, shy smile. The kiss was obviously playing through her mind again, just like it looped through mine.

"Strike that," Josh said. "I really don't want to know."

In the moments before the kiss, we'd been playing snap with that deck of cards. I'd accused her of cheating, mostly because she always did. About four months earlier, she'd found ways to use her boobs to distract me when she had a match. My accusation had led to a tickle fight—as it usually did. Which had somehow led to *that* kiss—which had never happened before. Although I'd had growing desires for something similar for a while.

When I met Alyssa's gaze again, the realisation that with one little kiss everything had changed struck with more ferocity. From that moment on, *everything* would be different. It had to be. There would always be the time before we'd kissed and the time after. I had no clue what that might mean for our friendship though. If things went badly, it could end nine years of being there for each other. Nine years of sharing everything with each other. Homework, dreams, desires.

Everything.

There wasn't a single detail of our lives we'd kept hidden from each other. Well, aside from my growing affection for her. I'd kept that secret because I'd thought that any relationship between us was off-limits. Still, she'd told me all about her first kiss with Blake. "Disgusting and slobbery," were the words she'd used to describe it. I only hoped I'd done a better job than he had.

In return, she knew about the many times I'd been rebuffed by Darcy Kinsley. Only days before, I'd spent half an hour whining to Alyssa about my continuing heartache over Darcy, and the fact that the blonde bombshell still didn't know I existed. Even then, I'd cared less about Darcy than I let on. Instead, it was the desire that had been growing second-by-second for my best friend which had overtaken my mind.

"Dad'll be home soon so Mum wanted me to find you," Josh said, after clearing his throat once more. "I had a feeling you would be here. But *that* I did not expect."

Is he pissed off?

I took the fact that I was still breathing as a positive sign. Even though he was her brother, he'd always been like a brother to me too. Our parents had always joked that they should just arrange joint custody, with the amount of time the three of us spent at each other's houses. Both sets of parents treated each of us as if we were their own children.

I'm sure that friendship was the only reason he hadn't ripped me from Alyssa's side and beaten me to a bloody pulp. After all, he had just witnessed me kissing his kid sister in a way that was anything but brotherly.

Considering that he had a good three inches on me, and was practically double my size in width, a wall of muscle already at sixteen, I really didn't want him to be pissed off with me. I dreaded to think the damage he might cause if he was.

"Five more minutes, Josh. I just want to talk to Declan alone for a sec." She brushed her hand through my hair, drawing my gaze back to her. I closed my eyes at the sensation.

"Sure, *talk*," Josh muttered. He did walk away and give us some privacy though, at least if we whispered.

"Um, okay, so what was that?" she asked me once he was out of earshot. The smile that played on her lips told me that despite the uncertainty in her words, she wasn't upset by the kiss.

I wasn't either, but I could hardly admit just how much I'd enjoyed it, or how much I wanted to do it again. At least, not until I knew she wanted it too. If she didn't, I had no idea where that left us.

"What, you attacking me?" I asked. A nervous chuckle escaped my lips as my stomach clenched at the thought of her lips on mine. *God, I want to do it again.*

"I seem to recall that you started it."

I wasn't sure that I had, but I couldn't say for sure that I hadn't either. True, I'd been the one to pin her to the ground when she'd refused to submit to my tickle torture. But in the seconds before our lips had touched, I'd had no control. It was as if some magnetic force had pulled us together during a brief lull in our laughter.

"That's not how I remember it," I said.

"I thought you still had a thing for Darcy?" she teased.

I raised an eyebrow at her. "Darcy who?"

Alyssa grinned at me.

Casting a quick glance over at Josh. I leaned closer to her so that my mouth was just centimetres from her ear. "To be honest, I really don't know who started *that*, but I'd like to spend a lot more time doing it. If it's okay with you, that is?"

A shiver raced through her as my breath raised a series of goose bumps on her neck. She grew breathless and nodded. Her voice was a hushed whisper when she said, "It's okay with me."

I cupped her chin and guided her lips back to mine. It was almost a chaste kiss—open-mouthed but no tongue. It wasn't the all-encompassing experience from earlier, but it was still damn good. It was still worth locking into my memories.

"Alyssa, will you be my girlfriend?" I asked when I dropped my hands away.

"Wow," she breathed.

Josh was starting to get impatient and paced back toward us. I cast him a quick glance, desperate to know what she thought before he was back with us.

"Wow isn't technically an answer," I teased, as I stood and offered her my hand. When our palms touched, she looked at me. I could see the same fears I had echoed in her eyes. To proceed would mean the end of our friendship as it had been. Then again, any friendship we'd shared was gone already anyway. It would be impossible to ignore the kiss that changed everything, which still blistered through me even without her lips on mine.

We shared two more shaky breaths before she answered. "Yes, but only on one condition."

I wondered what it could possibly be. My heart started to race as I imagined the countless demands that she might make in order for me to be with her. *Can I meet them?* "What condition?"

"That you'll be my boyfriend," she said with a teasing grin.

I laughed in relief. "Well, that's easy."

"C'mon, kiddo, before Mum starts to worry," Josh muttered, reaching for Alyssa's hand.

"One more second," she said, pulling free of his grip. Standing on her tiptoes, she pressed her lips to mine once more. My hand reached for the base of her neck to hold her close while I deepened the kiss. There was nothing chaste about it.

Josh cleared his throat and I reluctantly let go of Alyssa once more.

"Declan, you do know what I'll do to you if you hurt her." Even though Josh's words were designed to be threatening, the smile he wore was anything but.

Keeping my gaze focused on Alyssa, I answered Josh. "I know, man. But I could never hurt her. She's too important to me." As I said the words, I traced the curve of her cheek with my knuckles and met her eyes. I may have been answering Josh, but I was also reassuring Alyssa of the way I felt. I planted one more kiss on her lips and then whispered in her ear, "I'll call you later."

She smiled and gave me a small wave before following Josh out of the park.

I sat back on the grass, took a deep breath and let my imagination run wild. One thought seemed more important in my mind than any other at that moment: there would never be another girl for me. It seemed like a certainty branded onto every inch of my body.

I glanced in the direction Alyssa had just gone, wondering if her parents would mind one more for dinner again. On any previous evening, I wouldn't have even hesitated. Given what had just happened though, I decided to give it a miss for one night. Even though I was ready to see Alyssa again, I also wanted to remember the kiss for what it was. Most of all, I didn't want her to get sick of me just yet.

After cleaning up all of the playing cards I could find, and abandoning them in the park's rubbish bin because it was nowhere near a full deck any longer, I raced home. When I pushed the door open, I was ready for the lecture that Mum was sure to have prepared for me because I was so late. She would have already checked in with Alyssa's parents, Curtis and Ruth, and discovered I wasn't there. I could only hope Alyssa had told her parents that I was on my way home—even if I'd lingered at the park a little longer than I really should have.

"It's just me, Mum," I said as I threw my backpack down beside the front door, ready for the next day. There was some homework inside that needed to be done, but it would still be there in the morning. It was pointless trying to drag it out and do it then. After all, there was fat chance of concentrating on anything else as thoughts of Alyssa—of *kissing* Alyssa—danced in my head.

"Do I even need to ask where you've been?" Mum asked as I snatched a piece of carrot from her cutting board. She swatted me away but laughed as she did. After my last growth spurt, she barely came up to my chin, so it was easy to dart out of her reach with my prize still in hand.

"Not really." I jumped up onto the bench and threw the chunk of carrot in my mouth. With my newfound height, I was getting too tall to fit under the cupboards any more so I had to lean forward a little. The action of hopping up on the bench was habit though, and a bit of a routine for Mum and me. Despite how much she protested me parking my arse on the food-prep surfaces, it was clear she loved it when I sat and talked to her while she was cooking. Especially when Dad came home late from work.

She glanced up from her task. "And how is Alyssa?"

I couldn't hide the shit-eating grin my lips formed. "She's good."

Really good, I added in my head. *Especially at kissing.*

"What are you hiding?"

My grin stretched even wider. "I don't know what you're talking about."

The corners of her eyes pinched together. "Something's happened."

I rolled my eyes. "Why on earth would something have happened?"

Mum reached out and grabbed my chin, turning my head from side to side and assessing me carefully. "Because your darling baby blues are brighter than I've ever seen them before. Sparkling even," she teased, grinning.

After pulling away from her hold, I jumped from the bench. The more she confronted me about my afternoon, the less inclined I was to tell her about it. "I don't know what you mean."

She shrugged and shifted her gaze back to the vegetables she was chopping for dinner. "Keep your secrets then, but I need you to go get some milk."

"Sure. How long's dinner?"

Her lip pulled up to one side and her eyes—the same unique off blue, almost turquoise, colour as mine—danced toward blue in her amusement. "A metre and a half."

I snorted. "And you have the nerve to call me a smart-arse."

She shot me a glare, no doubt for my language—she couldn't stand the thought that I was getting older and she couldn't control the words I used anymore—and then glanced at the clock. "Well, if you will insist on using bad grammar, what can you expect? You've got about an hour."

I grabbed a handful of coins from the bowl on the end of the bench. "Okay, back soon."

After I'd left the kitchen, I heard Mum's voice calling after me.

"Declan?"

I backtracked. "Yeah?"

"You know parents have eyes and ears everywhere, right? I'll find out what it is you don't want to tell me." She raised her eyebrow at me in challenge.

I shrugged. "Well, I guess I don't have to tell you then, do I?"

Her eyes narrowed as she followed my logic. Feeling victorious, I walked away.

"Oh, and Dec," Mum called out again.

I backtracked again.

"Put your uniform in the laundry."

I laughed. "Sure thing."

After dumping my dirty clothes from my hamper into the laundry pile, I stopped back by the kitchen.

"Is Dad going to be home tonight?" I'd half decided to tell them both about Alyssa and me over dinner because there seemed little point having the conversation twice.

Mum jumped at the sound of my voice. "Haven't you left yet?"

I chuckled. "I'm going now. You didn't answer my question though."

"He'll be home late." She turned to me with narrowed eyes and her hands on her slender hips. "Why do you want to know?"

I shrugged. "No reason. Back soon."

Within ten minutes, I was at the small corner shop. Instead of heading straight inside though, I paused at the door. Lining the large window out front was a bank of novelty toy machines that grabbed my attention. Nestled among the modern machines was an ancient gumball-style machine that took twenty-cent pieces. That in particular caught my eye because it held a variety of toys, including hi-bounce balls, figurines, and a number of different-coloured plastic rings, hidden in clear plastic eggs. Near the top, I spotted a purple one and was struck by how perfect it would be for Alyssa. It was meaningless really, a bit of plastic junk, but I wanted to get her *something* to commemorate the day we'd shared our first kiss, and something to prove that I knew her well enough to know her favourite colour.

I fed the one twenty-cent piece I had into the slot and turned the dial. When the plastic container dropped into the prize shoot, I lifted the flap and checked to see what I'd got. A pink ring. Pretty enough, but not the purple one I wanted. I raced into the shop and changed the three one-dollar coins I had for fifteen twenties.

One after the other, I fed the coins into the machine and turned the dial. Each time, I got something else and not the ring I wanted. A little boy walked past, and I gave him a couple of hi-bounce balls, but I still had an array of them littered all around the area as well as five rings in different colours. With each coin I fed in, I got more frustrated, but also more hopeful. My logic was that the odds were better with every attempt.

Finally, with just two twenty-cent pieces left, I pulled a purple ring from a plastic container. I would have been elated if not for the fact that I had a pile of junk around me and no money left for the milk Mum had wanted. By the time I got home, grabbed more money, and then made it back to the shop, it'd be shut.

With a deep breath and a growing feeling of dread, I figured there wasn't much I could do but go home and face the music.

I left all the rings and hi-bounce balls that I didn't want on top of the machines, hoping some kids might grab them and put them to use after I'd gone.

Mum was waiting at the door when I got home. "Where have you been?"

"I went to the shop, remember?"

"Then where's the milk?"

"Um, well, about that." I tucked the ring between my fingers so she wouldn't see it. "I got a little sidetracked."

"With what, exactly?"

My face burned—I had no doubt I was turning red. "Nothing."

"Declan Anthony Reede." She didn't say more. She didn't have to. Her tone said everything.

"I just had to get something." I hung my head. "For Alyssa," I added almost silently.

"What did you have to get that could possibly be so important and take so long?"

I closed my fingers more tightly around the ring, the edges of the plastic digging into my skin.

"Declan." Mum's voice held a clear warning.

Without saying anything, I held out my hand and uncurled my fingers. Mum looked at the ring and then up at my face.

"Why on earth would you get her a toy ring?"

I attempted a smile, but it was hard with the weight of the guilt that I'd spent Mum's money on something that maybe was a little less important than I'd hoped it would be.

"Because she's my girlfriend?" I'd hoped the statement would come out assertive and strong, but instead my voice squeaked and I sounded more like I was asking a question.

Mum's eyes widened and then she chuckled. She shook her head and turned away.

"Finally."

I frowned. "What exactly is that supposed to mean?"

She spun back toward me and leaned against the back of the couch. "It means that I'm happy you two have finally woken up to the one thing that has been blindingly obvious to the rest of us for years now. You care about each other, and not just as friends."

"You didn't think to fill me in on this apparently obvious secret?"

She lifted one shoulder in a weird half shrug. "You had to come to the conclusion on your own. Both of you did."

My mouth hung slightly agape as I tried to process the fact that apparently everyone else knew Alyssa and I wanted to be more than friends, even though we'd only just realised it ourselves that afternoon.

"This doesn't get you off the hook though. Your dad isn't going to be able to have his coffee in the morning now. He won't be happy."

An urge to tell her that he could have juice instead built in me, but I bit my tongue to stop it. I didn't need to push my luck any further. As it was, I'd probably have my pocket money docked for the money I'd spent.

Luckily, I didn't have to face the music with Dad before going to bed. Just as Mum had said, he was late home so Mum and I had dinner alone. In fact, Dad still wasn't home by the time Mum shooed me off to bed.

Before I went to sleep, I put the plastic ring on my bedside table so I wouldn't forget it in the morning. Even though I knew I'd done something a little stupid, I couldn't regret the prize I'd won for Alyssa. There was no doubt in my mind that she'd love it. For the first time in ages, I was looking forward to going to school, if only for the chance to announce to our classmates that she was now my girlfriend.

The thought was enough to give me cause to relive the pleasure of her kiss, using the palm of my hand as a substitute for her body beneath me.

CHAPTER TWO

THE END OF AWKWARD

WHEN I WOKE, there was a weight on the end of my bed and someone speaking. Through half-opened bleary-eyes, I saw my father sitting near my feet. I couldn't believe he'd come into my bedroom uninvited. Mum had stopped doing that after interrupting an incredibly quiet and awkward moment by barging in unannounced.

Between his fingers, Dad held Alyssa's ring, occasionally twirling it around as if he were lost in concentration over it.

"Your mother told me what happened," he said when he saw I was awake.

"I told her I was sorry."

"You didn't actually."

"Well, she knows I meant to."

"I'm sure she does." He looked down at the ring again. "That's not really what I wanted to talk to you about though."

"Well, then what do you want? I've got places to be."

"Declan, I don't know what has gotten into you lately."

It was almost impossible to resist the urge to roll my eyes, but I managed somehow. I swear with every passing week Dad spent less time at home but somehow more time making demands of me.

"What exactly is this for?" He held the piece of purple plastic out to me.

Sitting up, I reached forward and snatched it from him. "It's just a present."

"Yes, for Alyssa. Your mum told me that. But why?"

My fingers traced a path through my hair. I really didn't need to be dealing with this shit first thing in the morning. "Because I wanted to buy her a present."

"But what for? You're not getting serious, are you?"

"Getting serious? Are you serious? I'm fifteen." Throwing my blankets off, I leapt out of the bed. I moved through my room with the intention of ignoring him while I organised my uniform for the day. I picked up a school shirt, unsure if it was dirty. With a sniff, I decided that clean or not, it was passable. When I saw he wasn't moving or saying anything further, I spoke again. "We're together, but God knows what that means."

He nodded solemnly and considered his hands for a moment. A second later, he spoke again. "Are you two being sexually active?"

"Jesus Christ, Dad."

He held his hands up in surrender. "Okay, I don't need you to tell me. Just promise me you'll be careful if you are, or if you do."

I was struck dumb by my disbelief that I had to have this conversation with him. Especially after he'd come into my bedroom without permission.

Dad took the hint provided by my silence, and moved to leave. He paused at the door. "You don't want to throw away your life before it's even begun. Just remember the dream we've been working toward. You've got a chance to make something of your life. Don't squander it by settling down too early."

His words caused me to pause.

A girlfriend would put a dampener on my long-term plans for a career in racing. But I was sure Alyssa would be different. She knew my dreams; she wouldn't stand in the way of them.

DESPITE DAD'S early morning attempt at *the talk*, his reminder of the potential cost of a girlfriend, and the fact that I had no milk for my cereal, my mood was practically euphoric when I left for school. There was so much for me to look forward to.

The plastic purple ring felt almost heavy in my pocket as I walked to Alyssa's house.

When I knocked on the door, I was greeted by the normal call of, "Hey, Dec," from three different voices and took that as a cue to head straight inside. The door was never locked on school mornings because they expected me at some point.

"Have you had breakfast?" Alyssa's mum, Ruth, asked when I reached the kitchen.

"No, we ran out of milk." I chuckled once the words were out.

"What's so funny?" Josh asked.

Ruth had already poured a bowl of cornflakes and placed them in front of me.

"Nothing," I said. "Where's Lys?"

"Still getting ready," Josh muttered. "Said something about needing to dress up for her new boyfriend."

Warmth spread through me at the thought. That was me. *I* was her boyfriend. Each new breath was a little harder to take than the last as an overwhelming sensation filled my chest. She wanted to look nice for me—*because* of me. Not that she didn't usually look nice. It was just that she was a bit of a tomboy, especially when it came to clothes and hairdos. That much had been clear from the very first time I'd met her.

WE'D BEEN just six when she'd moved from New South Wales to Queensland. Her boyish body was wrapped in a pair of short bike pants and an oversized t-shirt. When the teacher introduced her to us, her eyes watched the ground in front of her instead of meeting anyone else's gaze. Despite that, she held her chin up high. In the time since, I'd learned the second part was because she was so incredibly stubborn. She would never let anyone think they'd gotten the better of her. The contradiction struck me immediately.

It was the first day of school and the class was playing tunnel-ball as a way of getting to know each other. Because I'd won the game of continuous cricket we'd played the day before, I had been selected as one of the team captains. I took one look at her, with her plain clothes and her hair pulled into two unruly pigtails, and figured she had to be a tomboy and therefore good at sports, so I picked her first for my team. The look of immediate relief that crossed her face enamoured me of her completely. During that game, I discovered how uncoordinated she was, not to mention terrible at sports, but it didn't matter. From that day forward, I always picked her first when I was team captain.

In return, Alyssa had been there for me over the years. Like when we were ten and she'd come to my rescue on the playground. My sometimes friend, sometimes enemy, Blake Cooper, had spent the morning relentlessly teasing me for my not-quite-blue, not-quite-green eyes and fiery hair.

Over and over, he'd called me ranga until I'd finally snapped and leapt at him. We became a flurry of fists as I demonstrated the reason redheads had a reputation for being short-tempered. Instead of running off to the teacher, Alyssa had joined in the fray and copped an elbow to her lip. Hurt, she'd turned on the waterworks and sat on the edge of the sandpit, while the jerk Blake tried to apologise and blame me. Alyssa wouldn't accept his apologies though, demanding he say sorry to me instead.

When he refused, Alyssa stood, grabbed my hand, and led us away declaring, "C'mon, Dec. Who cares what that jerk thinks, I love the colour red."

There was also the time, just before my twelfth birthday, when I'd had my first proper girl-inspired boner over Darcy Kinsley's overnight breast enhancement—which I found out later was nothing but tissues and padding. Instead of laughing or telling the school about it, like I was certain Darcy would have, Alyssa distracted those around us so that I could make a quiet retreat.

Of course, she'd teased me about it after, but only once the bitter sting of my embarrassment had burned away.

We'd been there for each other through everything. The sort of friendship that seemed impossible to most people was second nature for us. Teasing one minute, sincere the next, but one thing was always constant—seeing Alyssa was always the highlight on my day.

SITTING IN her kitchen with her family surrounding me, the ring I intended to give her was burning a hole in my pocket. Maybe it was a stupid idea after all. Maybe she'd read too much into it, or think it was silly, or she'd just flat-out hate it.

I'd barely eaten the breakfast Ruth had laid out for me, even though I'd been starving when I'd arrived. There was no room for food around the knot that built in my stomach at a rapid rate. Despite the way we'd left everything the day before, the fact remained that it wouldn't be Alyssa-my-friend walking down the hall. Instead, I would be seeing Alyssa-my-girlfriend for the first time.

My breath caught as a lump grew in my throat to match the one in my stomach.

"Are you okay?" Ruth asked me. "You look a little pale."

"I'm fine," I said. My voice squeaked at the end, giving away my nerves.

A moment later, Alyssa's bedroom door opened and she came down the hall. I was relieved to see she looked relatively normal. Her hair was up in a ponytail like always and she wore the maroon-and-white uniform with a knee-length skirt like she always did. I had no complaints though. I liked her just as she was. I didn't need her to be someone new or different.

It was the little things that made her special to me. Like the fact that her legs were just a little on the skinny side, and her knees were just a little too big. Those things weren't flaws; they added character to her body. Her boobs formed two perfect mounds that looked like they'd be just the right size to fit into my palms, and my hands practically itched at the thought of testing the theory, especially now that there might be a chance I could. There was nothing about her I would have changed, even if I'd been given the choice.

In the end, all she'd done to dress up was run a slick of fairy-floss-pink lip gloss across her lips. I wondered whether it tasted like fairy floss too. I practically leaped from the stool at the breakfast bar and rushed to her side. Before I'd even thought about what I was doing, I pressed my lips to hers and stole a kiss.

It was only as I pulled away, licking my lips to taste the sweet candy flavour of her gloss, that I realised perhaps she hadn't told her mum about us yet. I clutched Alyssa's hand and turned back toward Josh and Ruth.

The grin on Ruth's face told me that either she already knew or she'd just assumed, like my own mother, that our relationship was inevitable.

"You coming, Josh?" I asked as Alyssa tugged me toward the door.

"No, I'd rather hang around here for a moment and keep my breakfast down than follow you two lovebirds to school."

"Suit yourself," Alyssa said with a laugh before pulling me outside.

Once we were alone on our way to school, she glanced down at our joined hands and then back up at me. Her wide smile and bright eyes told me she was feeling the same warm feelings I was.

"Hey, boyfriend," she said as she gave my hand a squeeze.

The shit-eating grin lifted my cheeks again. "Hi yourself, girlfriend."

"We probably shouldn't play hooky today, should we?" Without releasing my hand, she sped up a little before turning to walk backwards so that she could meet my eyes.

I thought about the day we could have if we did and ached to say yes. "We probably shouldn't. It's probably a better idea to prove we're going to be responsible even if we're a couple."

"Hmm, couple. I like the sound of it." She turned around again, resting her head against my arm as we walked.

I dropped her hand and wrapped my arm around her shoulders.

"Maybe we can still be responsible if we're a little late though?" she asked.

"Maybe. Why? What do you have in mind?"

She dragged me in the direction of the park where we'd played cards the day before—the park which had been "ours" for as long as I could remember and where everything had changed.

"Well, our first date was cut a little short, don't you think?"

The ghost of her lips tracing over mine filled my mind, together with the memory of her tongue tangling with my own.

"Definitely," I said, unable to keep the lust and desire from my voice.

We walked in silence until we arrived at our park. Without any verbal agreement, we made our way toward the table we'd claimed as our spot years earlier.

Alyssa sat on the bench and I took my usual place perched behind her on the table. I placed my legs on either side of her body and leaned my chin on the top of her head. It was a position we'd sat in hundreds of times before as we chatted about anything and everything. Only, this time it was different. Neither of us spoke, which had never really happened before. The silence around us was almost maddening; the only sound, our matching breaths.

"So—" we both said at the same time, before stopping at the same time.

"You go—" Again our voices were almost perfectly in sync.

I chuckled as she turned around and knelt on the bench to look at me. I helped her up onto the table beside me and just looked at her for a moment. Her lips called to me, and I wanted to kiss her, longed to with every part of me, but I didn't know if I should. I didn't want kissing to be the only thing we had. There was so much more that I liked about her and none of those things had changed. Yet it was still different. Everything was different.

"Don't hate me for asking, but is this weird as hell for you too?" she asked.

My relief that I wasn't the only one who was feeling the new, odd atmosphere surrounding us escaped in a quiet laugh. "*So weird.*"

"It shouldn't be though, should it?"

"No. I mean, we're still us, right?"

She practically leapt in place. "Right!"

"We're still friends," I added. "We always will be."

"Exactly. We're just friends that kiss now."

As she said the words, my gaze was drawn to her bright pink lip gloss. I licked my lips. "Friends that kiss a lot?"

"If you're lucky."

I trailed my hands into her hair, drawing her face slowly closer to mine. "Am I?"

"I don't know," she whispered. Her lips were so close to mine that I could feel her breath on my skin. "I'm starting to think that maybe I'm the lucky one."

I closed my eyes and covered the last of the distance between us in a heartbeat. Her lips were warm as they brushed against mine. Almost instantly, her tongue slipped into my mouth. My breath caught and my throat constricted. It would take some getting used to, being able to kiss her in that way.

"I'm definitely the lucky one," I said as we broke apart again. "And this"—I pressed my lips to hers again—"doesn't change anything between us. Okay?"

"Never," she whispered. "You're still my best friend, Dec. Nothing will change that."

"Good. Now, we'd better get going or we'll be late for school."

"It's the last week of the year. We could wag. No one would notice."

I shook my head. Although I really wanted to just go with her suggestion and forget about school for the day, I didn't want to do anything to make our parents think our being together would cause trouble. I jumped off the table and grabbed my bag. "Josh would."

"He wouldn't tell." She lay back on the table. The movement caused her school blouse to lift away from her stomach. I averted my eyes, something I'd never done before. It was all different now. I didn't know the rules when it came to ogling her now. I guessed I was allowed to because she was my girlfriend, but I didn't want her to think that she was my girlfriend only because of her *assets*.

"He might." I picked up her bag as well. "Not today, Lys. I don't want anyone giving us shit about us being together because we wagged the first day we were official."

As soon as I said the words, I was reminded of the little gift I'd bought for her to celebrate our first kiss. I dropped both bags to the ground and grabbed the ring out of my pocket.

"I almost forgot. I got you this." I held out the ring between two fingers.

"What is it?" She sat up and reached for it. "A plastic ring?"

Her gaze lifted, seeking mine. Her brows knitted together and her lips pursed.

The way she said it made me feel stupid, especially when I'd wasted Mum's money trying to get it.

"Why did you get me a plastic ring?"

"I thought you'd like it." My voice was a little icier than I'd intended, but I hadn't really anticipated that she would reject my gift.

"I do." The words were said almost as a question. She spun the ring around in her fingers. "I'm just not sure what it's for."

She held up her hand; the ring was on her pinkie finger, and didn't even fit all the way down to the first knuckle. A moment later, laughter escaped her.

"Seriously, it doesn't even fit my pinkie."

I stepped forward and snatched the ring back from her.

"Don't worry about it then," I said as I tossed it into the long grass that circled the park. "I thought that maybe I should get you something to commemorate our first kiss, but I guess I was wrong."

She scrambled off the table and looked at the place where I'd tossed the ring. "God, Dec, stop being such a drama queen."

"Well, if I'm such a drama queen, maybe the ring isn't the only thing I was wrong about." I ducked and grabbed my bag, slinging it over my shoulder before stalking off toward the school without looking back.

By the time I reached the school gate, guilt over the way I'd left Alyssa filled my stomach. I knew I was being overly dramatic, but I couldn't help it. There were times it felt like a switch had been flipped inside my brain. When that happened, I was set to autopilot and self-destruct all at the same time.

I turned around and headed back for the underpass, intending to walk back to the park and apologise. Instead, I met her halfway through the concrete tunnel.

"I was coming back to find you," I said.

"What the hell was that?" she said, with unmistakable venom in her voice.

"Do you know how much trouble I went through to get you a damn purple ring?"

She closed her eyes and sighed. "No, why don't you tell me?"

For the next few minutes, I ran through the story of the milk and the many attempts at getting that specific ring, the one in her favourite colour. By the end, we were both laughing.

"I don't understand you. You go to all that effort to get me a present and then you throw the damned thing away before I can even enjoy it."

"You didn't want it."

"If I didn't want it, would I have gone into that grass, even though I knew darn well it's going to give me hives, just to retrieve a hunk of plastic?"

"What?"

She held out her hand, the purple ring rested on her palm. Up the length of her arm splotches of red already marred her pale skin.

"Lys," I admonished. "You should have just left it."

"I didn't want to. Like you said, it's something to remember our first day together."

My lip twitched. "And now our first fight as a couple too."

"And the first time we kissed and made up." She touched her lips to mine.

"Hmm, I like the sound of that. Maybe we should fight more, just so we can have the making up kiss again and again?"

"Or we can just have the kissing without the fighting?"

"Where's the fun in that?"

She started to scratch at her arm.

I frowned. "Come on, let's get to sick bay and see if they've got anything to help with that rash."

CHAPTER THREE

THE END OF SCHOOL

DESPITE THE ROCKY start to the morning, our first day at school as a couple went better than I'd expected. Of course, Alyssa and I had to spend more time apart than we did together—we had very few classes in common. Although, being that it was the last week of school each class pretty much consisted of a rotation of movie marathons and various games.

Even my other best friend, Ben, was in more classes with Alyssa than he was with me. Instead, I had to put up with the blonde brigade—a group of two boys and two girls who tormented the school. Darcy Kinsley, Blake Cooper, Spencer Patterson, and Hayley Bliss: the kids who thought they were popular, who acted popular, but who were the butt of everyone else's jokes behind their backs. I got along with them all well enough generally, especially individually, but it wasn't as effortless as being with Ben or Alyssa. Especially not when all I wanted to do was find Alyssa and kiss her some more. It wasn't long before I realised I should have just let her convince me to ditch school for the day. We could have spent the day together. It wasn't like we were really needed there anyway.

"I'm going to ask Alyssa today," Blake whispered to Spencer

while they had their heads down on the desks behind me. It was in the middle of math class—and the latest round of heads down thumbs up.

His statement earned him my undivided attention.

"Dude, you've been saying that for two weeks now," Spencer replied with a laugh. "You'll pussy out today just like every other day."

"I haven't pussied out. Just decided to delay it. You saw what she was like last time. She just wants to get all serious and shit. I'm just looking for a proper make-out session in the back of the movies. Maybe even a chance to take a punt at second base."

Even though my forehead was on the desk and my eyes were closed, I could easily imagine the looks on their faces while they discussed my Alyssa. I clenched my fists.

Spencer chuckled. "Yeah, I could totally see her being a one man kind of girl. Not like Darcy. Man, I swear she'll chase anything with a dick."

When a finger brushed along my thumb, I almost leapt in my seat. The game had completely slipped my mind as I listened to the two bozos behind me chat in hushed whispers. I tucked my thumbs in and waited for Mrs. Turner to call time on the current round. Any guess I made would be exactly that—a guess. I didn't even try to concentrate on the touch, just on the conversation behind me. The only consolation was that once the bell rang for the end of this period, it would be lunch time and I'd see Alyssa again. And maybe we'd even announce our news to our small group of friends.

"ALYSSA!" BLAKE Cooper's shout pulled me from my thoughts.

For most of lunch, and while I waited with Alyssa by her classroom, I'd been lost in her beauty. It wasn't that I'd never noticed it before, I'd always thought her beautiful, but I'd just never really concentrated on all the finer details. Not really. It felt impossible for me to take my eyes off her now.

Blake's shout had interrupted my study of the swell of her lips.

Alyssa turned toward him with a slight smile on her face. His face lit up in return, and I knew the reason—his conversation with Spencer played in my mind.

A smirk played across my lips while I watched the scene play out. Because of the way we were standing, he wouldn't have seen the way Alyssa's hand joined with mine or the way my thumb stroked along hers. He hadn't realised he was already too late to ask her out again.

"What is it, Blake?" Alyssa asked. I could have imagined the trace of annoyance in her voice.

He closed the distance to where we stood fairly quickly. "Can I talk for a min . . ." He trailed off as he took in our pose and Alyssa's hand tightly clasped in mine.

His eyes flicked to mine and my smirk grew wider. I tried very hard to communicate with only my eyes. *Yes, fucker, she's mine now. You snooze, you lose.* To demonstrate my point, I kissed her lightly on the cheek, earning a blush.

Blake narrowed his eyes at me and I had to stifle a chuckle. Yeah, it was a ridiculous male ego thing, but I couldn't help but rejoice in the fact that Alyssa picked me over not only him, but over every other wanker in the school. I decided to show off just a little. I wrapped my arms tightly around Alyssa's waist and kissed her cheek again. "I'll catch up with you later. Okay, Lys?"

I didn't really want to leave, especially not with Blake sniffing around, but the bell had already rung for the next period and I still had to get to class. Unfortunately, Blake and Alyssa were in the same room, whereas I was on the other side of the school.

She turned to me and she kissed me hard on the lips. Her tongue snaked out and slid across my lower lip, tempting my tongue forward. I grinned at her when she pulled away. She was staking her claim as much as I had.

"Later, then," she said to me.

I walked off with a loopy grin on my face. It was amazing how easily Alyssa was able to affect me. If Alyssa's kiss made me smile though, the exchange I heard between her and Blake made me positively beam.

"So, you and Reede, huh?" Blake asked.

"Yeah." Alyssa was almost breathless.

"I don't like it."

"*You* don't have to." I could hear the bristle in Alyssa's voice. I risked one last glance back to see her brush past Blake and into the classroom. My grin was so wide it was almost painful.

BEFORE I knew it, the last few days of school had finished, the Christmas holidays had started, and summer was in full force. It would have been nice to say that my summer was filled with lazy days hanging with Alyssa and Josh, or even Ben, and not a lot else, but that wasn't the case. Like every other school holiday, I'd planned to spend hours and hours at the kart track. Only, when I woke the first weekend after school had let out, I had a surprise visitor—one of Dad's cousins, Dean.

Dean was . . . unique. For all of my life, he'd sworn that both he and my Dad could have been champions, up there with the greats of motorsport. For years, they'd raced together. Only, Dad had stopped racing before he was twenty, selling the car and leaving Dean, two years his junior, without a vehicle or sponsor and unable to continue in the sport. By the time Dean finally got back into it, he believed he was too old to make anything of himself. For years, he and Dad hadn't spoken but eventually he came around and started to support my karting career.

When I emerged from my room sometime around ten, he was sitting at the dining table with Mum and Dad.

"You still keen to get behind the wheel of something with a bit more grunt?" he asked when he saw me.

I brushed my hand through my hair and tried to act nonchalant even though I had a suspicion I knew where the conversation might be going. He'd talked a few times about letting me take his VK Commodore round the track on a hot lap or two. "'Course. Why?"

"I'm getting too old and too fat to get the VK around the track and I need someone a bit younger and hungrier to drive the season."

My eyes widened. It wasn't just what I'd hoped, it was better.

"You're shitting me?"

"Language, Declan," Mum admonished.

"Sorry, Mum." I gave her a sheepish smile before turning back to Dean. "You'll let me drive your baby?"

"She'll be your baby on the track."

"That's so awesome. When can I give her a go?" My face fell as I considered the fact that I couldn't go for my sprint series licence for another half a year—not until my sixteenth birthday.

"You can come with me now if you want? We've got some testing to do. It's not actual track time, but it'll get you behind the wheel for a while."

"What about licencing? I can't get my track licence for another six months."

"Let me deal with that," he said.

I had no idea what deals he was wheeling, but I wasn't going to argue if it got me proper track time. "Can I do it?" I looked to Mum to check it was okay. I didn't even bother checking with Dad; he'd been the one to push me into karting originally, even if Mum had been the one to drive me to every race, practice session, event, and test day.

"It's okay with me, just so long as you don't have any other plans today?"

"Just hanging with Lys, but she'll understand."

Half an hour later, I'd spoken with Alyssa—who was as understanding as I could expect considering I'd cancelled our plans minutes before I was due at her house—and was heading out to Ipswich with Dean.

Two hours later, Alyssa rang me.

"Are you going to be 'round tonight?" she asked after we'd gotten past the greetings.

I was only half listening to her because Dean was taking the car through her paces with me in the passenger seat. His driving lesson was light years away from the ones Mum had given me. Where she preached safety and caution, his only commandment was speed. Taking us into a back street in the industrial area which housed his garage, he threw the car into a series of doughnuts and figure eights. The momentum caused me to drop the phone. By the time I picked it up, Dean was silently asking if I wanted a go. Despite the fact that I didn't even have my learner's permit yet, I was eager. If he was willing to let me control his baby for a while, who was I to refuse? There was a risk we'd get caught by the police, but that would be on Dean—not me.

"Dec, are you even listening to me?" Alyssa's voice was cold as she tried to get me to pay attention to her again.

"Sorry, Lys. I've gotta go."

"When will I—"

I hung up before she finished the sentence and practically raced for the driver's seat. Sure I was going to cop hell for it later, but the chance at taking over the car with Dean's blessing was too hard to refuse.

For the next week, I split most of my days between Dean, learning the specifics of handling his VK Commodore, at the Willowbank drag strip—learning how to handle getting the car off the line as fast as I could—and the kart track, honing my skills ready for my first big race. Even though the kart track wasn't ideal, the race fundamentals, like picking the racing line, feeling the track, and knowing when to corner and how hard to brake, were somewhat universal.

By the end of the week, I had a special exemption provisional race licence. Dean mentioned something about it being a trial run. That the motorsport body was thinking of lowering the age to fourteen the following year to line up with other international rules. Apparently I was to be one of a handful of test cases across Australia, but I didn't listen to it all because I had my licence in my hand. That was all that mattered.

Despite how hard I had to practise for the next season of racing—in a car for the first time ever—I still had a little down time. Every spare second I did have was spent with Alyssa. Some days she'd come to my place, some we'd go to hers, but the best were when we'd meet at our park in the middle.

When the time I had spare grew from almost full days to less than an hour every couple of days, Alyssa complained about the lack of time we had together, I promised her something special for Christmas. Only, I didn't know what the hell that was going to be. My mind rolled with a thousand different possible presents to buy her to prove my loyalty.

We'd exchanged gifts for as long as I could remember, but it felt different buying for her as a girlfriend rather than just buying for a friend. I wanted our first Christmas as a couple to be memorable, so the usual presents just wouldn't suffice.

I'd read through all of the girlie magazines I could—hiding in the back corner of the newsagency of course, because there was no way I would let myself be seen buying them—and they seemed to be full to the brim of ideas at first glance. Most of the ideas just didn't seem right for her.

Perfume? I liked the way Alyssa smelled. I especially liked the scent of her coconut skin cream and fairy-floss lip gloss.

Jewellery? I had no idea what style she liked, and the limited funds I had to spend would only go far enough to buy her crap that would probably tarnish and break in no time.

Gift card? Too impersonal.

Lingerie? Too personal. Plus, I got a boner every time I even walked past the shop.

Other clothing? It meant taking a wild guess on shape, colour, style, and size. Too hard to get right, and far too dangerous to get wrong.

I searched high and low before deciding on the perfect gift for her— on the last shopping day before Christmas. It represented the three things I wanted to shower her with: my heart, my time, and my love.

Christmas came and went, and I gave Alyssa a photo book of all my favourite pictures of us. Even though I had worried she might think I was just being cheap, she seemed pretty cool about the gift. I wondered whether that was because she could tell I had a little more planned.

On Boxing Day, I had Josh drive Alyssa to the Grand Plaza and drop her at the food court. I met her there, presenting her with two tickets to see a movie. I didn't really pay much attention to the screen, I couldn't. Not with Alyssa beside me.

Throughout the movie, I kept distracting her with my desperate need to kiss her and touch her. She never stopped me though, so I assumed she didn't mind. After the movie, we wandered the shops for a while. When we passed Kmart, I asked her to wait while I ducked inside. After grabbing what I needed, I came back out and offered her the rest of my gift: a chocolate heart and a calendar.

She offered me a confused look as she thanked me for them.

"It's the three things I want you to have more than anything. My time, my heart, and our future."

The burgeoning smile on her lips and the tears welling in her eyes proved that the sentimental shit meant more to her than the most expensive present in the shop. I wrapped my hand around hers, "C'mon, let's walk back to mine."

CHAPTER FOUR

THE END OF THE FIRST TIME

UNLIKE OUR FIRST Christmas as a couple, our first Valentine's Day was a disaster.

Even though we'd been dating for about four months, and everyone in the school knew how intense we were about each other, some weren't happy with it. Blake constantly sniffed around Alyssa, waiting for me to screw things up, and Darcy had been trying to cause a fight between me and Alyssa ever since the school year had started again at the end of January. I'd heard rumours that her plan was to sweep in after the fact, play the good friend, and get the man. It was stupid really, and more than a little ironic, that by the time she was finally interested in me, being with her was the last thing on my mind.

I had no real clue why Darcy had developed her sudden attraction, other than the fact that I was off-limits and no longer interested. Spending so much time training and at the track probably didn't hurt my case either. The extra work had grown the muscles across my arms and chest, causing them to swell and firm in a way that was appreciated, certainly by Alyssa.

When the bell rang for lunch, I headed up to the racks at the front of the classroom to grab my bag. Shoved underneath the backpack was a huge pink envelope. I grinned as I reached for the card, assuming it was Alyssa doing some over-the-top gesture for Valentine's.

Darcy moved straight to my side, her fingers twirling in the ends of her blonde hair. "What's that?"

I rolled my eyes as I grabbed the card. "What does it look like?"

"It looks like someone got a Valentine. Is it from anyone special?"

"What do you think?"

Darcy leaned against the port racks, thrusting her chest out as if I might actually be interested in her because of the action. "I think maybe you should open it."

I put the card back on top of my bag. "I'm not going to open it here in front of everyone."

Grinning, she leaped forward and grabbed it from me. "Wait. It's got my name on it."

"What the hell are you talking about?" I snatched it back.

She twisted it in my hand. "It's got my name on it. See?"

I glanced down at the card in my hand with a frown. It did have her name on it. I had no clue why it was under my bag, though. Her books were in a metallic pink backpack, mine were in a Holden bag, to represent my true racing colours. It wasn't like the bags would be easily mixed up.

With a feeling of suspicion that there was something else happening that I didn't understand, I handed it back to her. "Well, if it's yours . . ."

When it was in her hands, she looked around at the little crowd that was gathering around us. Not only the students from our class, but also from the classroom beside us and the ones whose next class was in our room as well.

"Should I open it?" she asked, lapping up the attention. Her voice was too sugary sweet, and it made my suspicions grow even further.

Everyone nodded, no doubt waiting to see which hapless sap

wanted to be Darcy's Valentine.

"It's yours isn't it?" I shrugged and grabbed my bag.

She tore open the envelope. "Oh my God, Declan!"

I stopped mid turn as she said my name. The tone of her voice screamed danger.

"What?" My voice was ice as I turned to look at her.

Her body collided with me and her arms wrapped around my neck. She managed to kiss my cheek before I pushed her off. "I can't believe you got me a Valentine."

"What?"

A murmur of surprise went through the crowd and I could already hear the gossip mill as it started to grind.

"Darcy, I didn't—"

Darcy smiled as she looked over my shoulder. "Oh, sorry, Alyssa. I didn't see you there."

I spun around to meet Alyssa's gaze. The frown on her face told me she'd read the worst into what she'd just witnessed. She huffed out a breath, spun on her heel, and stalked away.

"C'mon, Lys, you can't be serious," I called after her.

Before I could give chase, Darcy grabbed my arm.

"She's a lost cause," she oozed. Her fingers trailed into my hair. "I knew you liked me. I was just silly for not realising sooner that I wanted you too."

I pulled my head away from her touch. "Piss off."

She raised an eyebrow at me. "Wow that hurts, coming from the guy who just gave me a Valentine."

"I'm guessing you set that little scene up," I hissed at her. "But it won't help you, Darcy. I *may* have had a crush when I was younger and stupider, but I will never want to be with you."

She stood blinking at me. "I don't know what you're talking about, Dec."

I could have stood arguing with her, but the more time I spent with her, the farther away Alyssa would get. Without looking back at Darcy, I chased after my girl.

When I caught up to her, I grabbed her arm to stop her from running from me again.

"What are you doing, Lys?"

"You didn't expect me to hang around and watch that display, did you?"

"You know I didn't give her that card."

She rolled her eyes. "I know that, Dec. I'm not stupid. I'm pissed that you let her make a scene like that. Do you know how many people saw that? How many people don't know what that cow has been doing, and will think that you actually gave her a card?"

Her logic didn't make any sense. Even though she knew I hadn't given Darcy the Valentine's Day card, she was still pissed at me. "So?"

"I just can't believe you'd be stupid enough to let her do that to you. To us."

"So I'm stupid, am I?"

She tugged out of my hold. "If the shoe fits."

"What exactly did you expect me to do?"

After making a sound filled with frustration, she paced a short distance away before spinning back toward me. "How about rip the card up the instant you saw it?"

"I thought it was from you, Lys, otherwise I would have."

"Why would I have left you something like that?"

By now a crowd had gathered around us, mostly eighth and ninth graders snickering at the lover's tiff between two eleventh graders. Their presence just served to piss me off more and I took it out on Alyssa. "I don't know, maybe because I thought you actually cared or that just maybe you'd want to give me a Valentine's Day card. I guess I was wrong, huh?"

"Of course I do, but I thought I'd give it to you in private." She glanced around at everyone nearby, retreating into herself at the attention. "I'm starting to wonder if you even know me at all."

"Don't be stupid, of course I do."

"Don't call me stupid."

I threw my hands in the air and groaned. "You called me stupid."

"Because you were acting stupid."

"God, stop being so stupid!" I reached out for her and tugged her into my arms. "Alyssa, you're the one that I want. The *only* one I want. Will you just be my goddamn Valentine?"

She rolled her eyes and huffed before tugging free of my hold. "Well, with an offer like that, how can I possibly refuse?"

Before we had a chance to finish the conversation, Mrs. Turner saw us out of class and came out of her room to shoo us along.

Alyssa shot me a glare and I knew it wasn't over.

After school, I couldn't find Alyssa anywhere. She wasn't waiting in our usual place. Around me, other kids rushed toward the oval.

I grabbed one of the tiny eighth graders as they raced past. "What's happening?"

"There's a catfight on the oval. Some chick dragged another down there by her hair." He practically leapt with joy as he pulled from my hold and kept running toward the bottom of the school.

Although I couldn't say how I knew, I was certain Alyssa was involved. It was the only explanation I had for why she'd failed to meet me. I raced toward the back of the school with everyone else, hoping she could hold her own until I got there.

When I reached the oval, the fight was all but over. Alyssa had Darcy's ponytail curled in her fist and was dragging her around the grassy area. Along Darcy's cheek was a scratch that could only have come from Alyssa.

I approached the pair with caution, trying to catch Alyssa's eye.

"Call off your dog, Declan!" Darcy shouted at me.

Alyssa gave a primal cry and yanked Darcy's hair. "Say that again, bitch."

"Lys," I said, drawing her attention to me. "Is she really worth getting in trouble over?"

"You should have heard her going on about the Valentine's card she pretended you got her, Dec. She's a fucking scrag!" Alyssa punctuated her sentence with a tug on Darcy's hair.

"But she's really sorry for her stupidity, isn't she?" I bent over to talk to Darcy, trying to warn her with my tone that the only way she was getting out of Alyssa's hold would be if she cooperated with me.

She rolled her eyes and didn't say anything.

Alyssa pulled her hair again. "He asked you a question."

"Let go of me, you cow!"

"You're really sorry, aren't you?" I gave the idiot another chance to apologise.

"Fuck you!"

I laughed. "Yeah, that's never going to happen."

She growled and pulled against Alyssa's hold, which only managed to pull her hair more.

"I'm going to tell you how this is going to go, okay? You can either agree, or I can leave you here with Lys."

Darcy growled at me like the dog she is. Throwing my hands up in the air, I walked away.

"Fine. Fine!"

I moved back toward the pair. "What's going to happen is that Lys will let you go, you'll get it through your thick head that Lys and I are together and happy, and you'll leave us alone from now on. Okay?"

"Fine!" Darcy cried. Once the words left her mouth, Alyssa let go of her hair and gave her a shove.

"Alyssa Dawson, my office. Now," Mrs. Turner snapped before turning and heading for the English block.

Neither Alyssa nor I had seen the head of the English department approach the oval, but it was clear she'd seen the fight or at least enough of it to present a damning case.

"I'm sorry," I mouthed before Alyssa spun on her heels and followed the teacher.

I stalked behind the pair of them, keeping just enough distance that I didn't draw attention to myself.

"Mr. Reede, I'm sure your parents will be expecting you soon," Mrs. Turner said when she spun to open the door for Alyssa. "Unlike Miss Dawson's, I won't be calling yours to escort you home."

Knowing there was little point hanging around the school unless I wanted to get in trouble myself, I headed straight to our picnic table and waited for Alyssa to meet me.

For at least two hours, I sat on the bench, paced the length of the park, and generally loitered, while keeping an eye out for her. When she never showed, I headed straight to her house. It was already dark by then, and I knew Mum was probably having kittens, but I needed to find out what had happened. I needed to know that Alyssa was okay.

When I knocked on her door, Josh answered it.

"Huh, I guess I lost my bet. I didn't think you'd be by tonight," he said by way of greeting.

"Why wouldn't I be? I wanted to check that Lys was all right."

"Well, Lys doesn't want to see you."

"Don't be ridiculous. Just tell her I'm here, will you?"

"Can't, man. She's grounded and not allowed to speak to you."

I leaned against the doorframe. "You just said she didn't want to, now you're saying not allowed. Which is it?"

"A bit of both. Mum and Dad aren't overly impressed with her little fight today and think you two need some space for a while."

"I don't want space. I want to see Alyssa."

"Sorry." He didn't sound very apologetic as he shoved me off the doorframe and then slammed the door in my face.

"Are you fucking kidding me right now?" I knocked on the door again. After no one answered, I knocked again.

The door swung open, but this time Curtis, Alyssa's dad, filled the frame. "Go home, son."

"I just want to speak to Alyssa."

"She made it pretty clear to us that she doesn't want to talk to you."

"Please?"

"You can see her tomorrow. She's grounded for her little stunt, but I'm sure we can give her a little leeway if you drop by for a few hours."

"I can't. I have a race tomorrow."

"Can't help you then, son."

I grunted in frustration.

He chuckled. "Maybe come by for dinner."

I said a cursory goodbye and let him shut the door before walking around to the outside of Alyssa's bedroom. I tapped against her window.

"Lys, are you there?" I whisper-shouted.

I heard a bump and a scrape from inside. She was definitely in her room. All I had to do was convince her to come to the window.

"Please, Lys?"

She drew back the curtains, but didn't open the window. She pressed a note against the glass which just read, *Go away.*

I shook my head. "Not until you talk to me."

She rolled her eyes but opened the window. "What do you want?"

"I want to make sure you're okay."

"Besides being grounded and suspended, you mean."

A chuckle escaped my lips before I had the good sense to stop it.

"Ugh," she groaned before moving to slide the window closed again.

"Wait, Lys, why don't you want to talk to me?"

"Why do you think?"

"I really don't know." I pressed my face against the window screen. I wished it wasn't there. I probably could have climbed into her room and convinced her not to be mad at me with my lips.

"If you hadn't been stupid enough to fall for Darcy's stupid trick, I wouldn't be grounded right now."

"Well, I didn't tell you to fight her."

"You just don't get it."

I frowned. She was so unreasonable sometimes, and it just made no sense. "No, I really don't."

She rubbed her temples as if talking to me was exhausting her. "This could ruin my chances to get into the uni courses I want to do."

"I don't think the school will let it get that far, will they?"

"They might not have a choice. Darcy's father threatened to press charges unless the school dealt with the matter."

"He can't do that. Can he?"

"It doesn't matter if he can or not. The school decided to suspend me. That sort of shit follows you around, Dec. And it's your fault."

"My fault?" I snapped. "How the fuck do you figure that? I didn't tell you to fight her."

"What other choice did I have?"

"You could have ignored her."

"Says the guy who threatened to bash Blake just for asking me to sign his yearbook."

"That was different."

"How?" Alyssa crossed her arms over her chest. I knew I was skating on thin ice, but I had no clue why. "How is it different?"

"Fuck! It just is."

"I don't want to talk about this now. Come back tomorrow when I've had time to calm down."

"I can't."

"Why not?"

"I've got a race. You know that."

"One day, Dec, you're going to have to choose between the damn karts and me."

I frowned as Dad's warnings came back to the surface. She would cost me my dream. Taking a deep breath, I pushed the thoughts back down. *Lys is different. She knows how much this means to me.* "It's not a kart race, it's at Queensland Raceway. In Dean's VK. My first proper race."

Because Dean lived at Ipswich, he maintained the car but I was free to use it for the race season. She knew how big a deal it was to me; a few days earlier she'd been bouncing with excitement for me.

"Same difference."

I frowned. "No. It's really not."

"Yes. It really is. Either way, you're picking a pile of metal and gears over me."

"It's not like that."

"Well, it sure feels like it. Come back tomorrow, Dec, or don't bother coming back at all." She slid the window shut, yanked the curtains closed, and ignored my attempts to coerce her back to talk some more.

When I arrived home, Mum was waiting by the door. "Where on earth have you been?"

"I don't want to talk about it." I pushed straight past her.

"Declan Anthony Reede, if you take one more step before explaining where you were, you will be grounded until you're twenty-five."

I didn't want to talk about it. I didn't want to listen. The only thing I wanted to do was lock myself in my room and play my music until my ears threatened to bleed. It was the only way to stop thinking—which was the only way to stop hurting.

Behind me, Mum continued her tirade, but I didn't listen. When I reached my bedroom, I slammed the door shut behind me and shifted my bed to brace the door so Mum couldn't follow me.

When she shouted at me to get out and speak to her, I just turned my music up louder.

The next morning, I woke and got ready for a day on the track. I'd spent the night planning it out. If I was ready for the track when I went to see Alyssa, I might be able to balance both tasks.

I walked into the kitchen for some breakfast.

"I don't know what you're dressed up for," Mum said. Her tone was still sharp. She was obviously still upset about the previous evening.

I frowned at her. She knew the importance of the race. "I have the first championship race today."

"You were given the car on the proviso that you did well at school and acted responsibly."

"And?"

"And your behaviour yesterday wasn't responsible."

"Fuck. It's not like I made Darcy that Valentine, or forced Alyssa to fight her."

"Language! And what are you talking about?"

"The fight. Lys calling it off. Everything going to shit. Isn't that what you mean?"

"I'm talking about the disrespect you showed me. I could almost have accepted you turning up here as late as you did without letting me know you weren't coming home, but the rest of it?" She assessed me for a moment before sighing and sitting at the table beside me. When she spoke again, her tone was softer. "It sounds like there is more you need to tell me though."

She waved her hand for me to tell her more.

We sat at the dining table and I told her about everything with Alyssa and Darcy, and the stupid Valentine that caused all the trouble. In the end, she agreed that there were enough extenuating circumstances to allow me to race, but that I was on my last warning. By the time we'd finished our chat, there wasn't enough time to see Alyssa before I left for Queensland Raceway.

I only hoped that Alyssa would understand.

CHAPTER FIVE

THE END OF IDIOCY

THERE WAS NOTHING worse than seeing Alyssa dating someone else.

After I'd apparently proven to her that I didn't care for her at all, that I'd rather have a race car than a girlfriend, she'd refused to take me back.

It killed me because I couldn't even talk to anyone about it. Ben had just started dating Alyssa's friend, Jade—they'd got together over a fucking Valentine of all things, and the only other person I wanted to talk to was exactly the person I wanted to talk about. My chest ached each time I saw her, but I couldn't do a damned thing about it. For the first two weeks, she'd refused to talk to me at all.

Eventually, she'd grown civil toward me, but that was it. I was granted precious few words. "Hello," "Goodbye," and the occasional, "How are you going?" but that was it. After two torturous months of living in limbo, waiting for the day she'd finally talk to me like we used to again, I found out that she'd accepted Blake's offer of a date.

After that, the two of them paraded around the school holding hands and I swear she'd kiss him every fucking time she saw me. Each time, my throat would clamp shut and my eyes would sting.

To pay Alyssa back for dating Blake-the-asshole, I even tried my luck with Darcy. It lasted a week. All she wanted to do was make out and there was nothing enjoyable about kissing her. It was all kinds of wrong, and not at all like it felt with Alyssa. Plus, I missed the conversations I'd shared with my best friend between the snogging sessions.

Instead of worrying about it when everything went to crap with Darcy, I threw myself into racing. I spent every weekend at the kart track or at Queensland Raceway. I even convinced Dad to take me to Willowbank for the drags on a few Saturday nights. He seemed happier after the breakup, telling me that I didn't need Alyssa in my life, not if she wasn't going to support me in pursuing my dreams.

By June, I heard through Josh that Blake and Alyssa had broken up.

Not that I cared. Or asked about her at all.

After their breakup, Alyssa started to hang around with Jade again. Which meant she was hanging out with Ben, and therefore me, again. Whenever the four of us were together, Alyssa's gaze would slide to look at me before shifting away the instant she was caught. A heaviness rested on her brow, so she walked around the school with an almost constant frown.

The air between us was awkward, stilted in a way it had never been before. Being in her proximity made my skin feel too tight and my heart ache like it was three sizes too big for my chest.

After three weeks of the same stilted, awkwardness, I couldn't cope anymore. I found someone else to sit with at lunch each day and watched Alyssa from a distance. When I got home, I just couldn't sit still at all. I had energy to burn so Mum sent me out of the house. Each evening, I found a new direction to walk.

When I came home from school on the last Friday of school before the June holidays, Mum shooed me from the house as usual even though it was my birthday.

Without even thinking about where I was going, I headed to

the park where I'd shared so many happy memories with Alyssa. We'd spent every birthday together for as long as I could remember. When I realised where I was, I dropped my head as the loss of the time with my best friend echoed keenly through my body. It wasn't the physical stuff I missed—although I did long for that too—it was the familiarity and the comfort she offered simply by being at my side. Shuffling forward, I didn't even notice Alyssa sitting at our table until I was practically on top of her.

"Hey," I said with a nod as I debated whether to simply keep walking. It would be easier to pretend I hadn't planned on sitting there and reliving the way things had been before we'd made the leap to boyfriend/girlfriend.

"Hey, Dec," she said as she slid over to make room for me to sit. Her voice was filled with sorrow and a heaviness I wanted to soothe away. I just didn't know how.

When I studied her face in the dusk, I saw tears tracking slowly down her cheeks.

"Happy birthday," she added.

I climbed onto the table beside her. "What's up?"

She shook her head and swiped away her tears. "Nothing."

"C'mon, Lys, I know you. Something's up."

She hung her head, letting her hair fall in curtains around her face.

"It's nothing," she said, but her voice was filled with fresh tears.

Without thinking, I moved closer to her and wrapped my arm around her shoulders. "I know it's not nothing."

She leaned into my hold before clutching at my shirt and pressing her face to my chest. "I miss you, Dec. I miss everything about you. I miss this. I miss *us*."

I closed my eyes and held her tightly, both arms wrapped around her body. Her words echoed my own thoughts almost perfectly. My chin rested on the top of her head, just like always. The movement was so familiar, so comfortable.

"Me too," I croaked out as best as I could.

"I'm sorry. I was an idiot. Can we try all of this again?"

I reached my finger underneath her chin, lifting her head so that I could claim her mouth.

"Of course," I murmured before moving in to kiss her.

She pulled away at the last second. "Shit. No. I don't mean that. Last time we tried that, everything went wrong. I just meant friends. Can't we be friends again? I don't like not having you around."

Her words shot through me like an arrow and I dropped my arms away from her. Turning away so she couldn't see the impact of her rebuff, I nodded. "Sure thing, Lys. I've got to get home though."

I jumped off the table, and didn't miss a stride before heading back to my house. It was a damn good thing the sun was setting so early lately and the sky was already darkening—it meant she couldn't see the way my cheeks burned.

"Dec, wait."

Closing my eyes, knowing without doubt I was powerless to resist her call, I stopped. I heard her footfalls behind me, and then she grabbed my arm and spun me around.

"You don't want to be friends again, do you?"

I shook my head. "No, Lys. I really don't."

Her expression fell, and a tear slipped from her eyes.

"I don't because I want more than that. I want what we had before Darcy pulled that stupid stunt and we let her get between us." I took her hands in mine and guided them to my chest so she could feel the way my heart raced when I was near her. "I want you, Alyssa. Not as a friend, but as more. You are *always* going to be more to me."

"Just promise you won't hurt me, Dec."

Even though I could have taken the chance to remind her that she'd been the one to do the hurting, that she'd been the one who'd decided not to be with me because of a stupid argument, I didn't. It might have broken whatever magic spell was guiding her back into my arms.

"I promise. I'll never be an idiot again." I grabbed her around the waist and swept her up to claim her lips.

CHAPTER SIX

THE END OF THE RACE

WE HAD TWO perfect weeks of school holidays, where Alyssa and I could just be alone together. It ended too soon.

Within a month, as the cold set in around us, we'd broken up again. I'd refused to talk to her after she'd gone to the movies with Blake and the blonde brigade, and hadn't invited me along. By August, we'd found our way together again. Even when September melded into October, we'd repeated our same destructive pattern. We'd only just gotten back together, when the most important race of the ProV8 series threatened to derail us once more.

Bathurst. An eight-hour trial by fire of the premium drivers in their million-dollar cars. I'd never missed watching a single one. Ever.

It was only half an hour before the big race was due to start, and I was still running around like a blue-arsed fly. Usually, Ben would have been at my house by then. We'd have already had eight hours' worth of snacks and drinks set up at the ready so we would only have to move from our seats for piss-breaks. It was the way we'd spent the Bathurst race every year, but this year he was being a pussy and spending the day with Jade. I was just glad that Alyssa understood that this was one race I couldn't miss.

Placing the esky on the table, filled with ice and drinks, I took a moment to breathe and assess my temporary man cave. It was perfection; a junk food heaven. Usually I tried to be mindful of what I ate, but Bathurst was the one day I indulged. My logic was that in a few years, when I was the one on the track, I'd be able to remember the influx of calories to get me through. Maybe it wasn't very logical really, but it gave me an excuse to have a guilt-free day of freedom.

I'd just settled into the spot on the couch which would house me for the next eight hours when there was a knock on the door. The cars were already out on the grid, and there was no way I was getting up again, so I called out for Mum. It was unnecessary in the end because she was already on her way to the door.

"Heaven forbid you miss a single minute of the race," she said as she walked behind me.

"I'm glad you understand," I said, making her laugh.

I turned my attention back to the TV as she greeted whoever it was that should have been parked at home watching the sacred race.

"I didn't expect to see you here today," I heard her say. The statement was enough to pique my curiosity and I listened more intently. "I thought you had plans."

My mouth lifted into a grin. I should have known Ben wouldn't back out of our man-date, not for Bathurst.

"So, did you demand Jade give your balls—" I turned away from the TV to greet him properly, but met Alyssa's unimpressed gaze instead. "Oh, shit, sorry, Lys." I turned back toward the TV, but slid over to give her some room beside me. "What are you doing here?"

"Nice, Dec. I thought I'd come see what all the fuss is considering I knew you'd be here alone, but if it's going to be easier for you, I'll just go."

I was torn. On one hand, it was the first time—*ever*—that she'd shown any interest in cars or watching a ProV8 race, but on the other, I didn't want to spend my day explaining the rules, the teams, the cars, and every other little detail that she could ask about. Not for Bathurst--the sort of race which could be won or lost at any second. There were rumours flying that it would be my idol, Sinclair Racing's Dane Kent's, last Bathurst ever, and I didn't want to miss a minute of the action. With him and the team's newest driver, Morgan McGuire, behind the wheel, they were promising to be the team to beat.

"No, Alyssa, please don't go, I really, really want you to stay," Alyssa said in a half-mocking tone, pulling me from my thoughts.

Her words could have easily pulled a foul mood from me, and on most days might have, but it was Bathurst, so not much could faze me. "See, I didn't need to say anything because you read my mind." I laughed and held my arm out to invite her to sit beside me.

She nestled under my arm, before looking over the spread I'd laid out for myself.

"I don't think I've ever seen so much junk food in one place outside of a supermarket," she teased.

"It's an eight hour race, baby." I grinned. "Gotta keep up my stamina somehow."

"Eight hours?"

"Well, the race itself is a little less than that, but with the start and the podium, it's about that long."

"Eight hours of watching the same cars go around the same track?"

I rolled my eyes. *Here we go.* "Yeah, it's an endurance race. The point is to stick it out to the end, it becomes about the asset management and pit crews as much as the drivers. It's racing at its finest."

She waved her hand dismissively. "Do you really have to watch the whole race then?"

I pulled away from her to check if she was being serious. "Of course, it can change in the blink of an eye." *If you don't wanna watch it, there's the door.* I bit back on the words because we'd been broken up until so damn recently that I was willing to give a little to be with her. Still, some of her comments made it pretty hard.

"So—"

Holding my hand up, I silenced her. "The race is starting." I sat forward, anxious to see whether Kent could get a good jump off the line.

"So—" she started again.

I spun to cast her a quick warning glare. The start of the race was vital, with everyone jostling to be the first off the line. Although the first corner wasn't vital like it was for shorter races at other tracks, it was easily the most exciting corner. With the exception of the last. She held up her hands in surrender and pretended to lock her lips as she rolled her eyes.

My breath was caught tight in my chest as I watched, ready for the jump. It was too easy to imagine what it must be like for the drivers. The excitement; the thrill of the chase; the noise and feel of the car rumbling beneath them. I'd experienced that in karting, and more recently in the VK, but I was sure it was barely one-tenth of the thrill of handling one of those beasts. When the green flag went up, I perched forward in my seat, willing Kent's car to go.

He lurched off the line from pole position and surged forward. The Ford driver, Hunter Blake, bit his heels, but Kent arrived first and made it through clean. Positions four and five hit the corner at the same time and touched door handles, but kept control over their cars. With relief that Sinclair had such a good start, I sagged back into the couch, ready to relax into an awesome day of petrol-head fun.

"That's it?" Alyssa asked.

"What do you mean?"

"That's what I needed to be quiet for?"

"Yeah. I needed to concentrate."

She laughed. "You know you're not driving the car, right? You have zero control over anything that is happening."

"One day I will though."

With a roll of her eyes, she turned away.

"I will, Lys, just you watch me."

She offered me an indulgent smile. "I know that's the dream."

Ignoring the race, I turned to her. "No, it's not."

"Huh?" she asked, teasing her fingers through my hair.

"You say, 'the dream' like it's something that won't happen. This *will* happen."

"You've still got another year of school left though."

"Yeah?"

"You might change your mind by then."

It was my turn to offer an indulgent smile. Sometimes, it was like she didn't know me at all. Deciding it wasn't worth the argument, I settled into the seat and invited her to snuggle into me.

The silence lasted three laps, and then Alyssa started to ask about my plans for Christmas, for a double-date with Ben and Jade, and for a whole heap of other things that I didn't really care about while the cars were on the track. "Lys, can you at least wait for the ads?"

She gave me a look of innocent confusion.

"I'm trying to watch the race."

She rolled her eyes, but stopped talking and shifted so that she was lying on the couch with her head in my lap. I smiled when she rolled over to watch the TV, seemingly interested in the race.

Then she yawned and rolled back over to glance up at me. "Can't we go for a walk or something?"

"I'm watching the race." I was certain I'd failed to keep the irritation out of my voice.

"But there's hours to go, right?" She reached up and stroked my face before tickling her fingers over the skin of my neck. "Can't we go for a walk and come back closer to the end of the race?"

"But then I'd miss the race."

"Not the end. That's the important bit isn't it?"

"I don't think you understand how it works."

She sat up and pressed her lips to mine. "C'mon, let's go do something."

I pushed her away gently. "Lys, please."

She huffed and sat on the opposite end of the couch. When I was certain she wasn't looking, I rolled my eyes. It was exactly the reason why I hadn't invited her over. It was impossible for her to understand how important every single lap was. There were so many different things that could shape the race in an instant: someone pitting early—or late, a safety car, the weather, overtaking, or even brake failure. At any stage, a driver could make a critical error. If I left, and then came back for the last fifteen minutes, I'd have to spend that whole time scrambling to figure out who was where and what had happened.

Without words, I stood and headed for my bedroom. When I passed the door to Mum and Dad's room, Mum looked up from her book and gave me a questioning look. I just shook my head to tell her not to ask.

After grabbing my laptop from the dresser, I turned around and headed straight back to Alyssa. I tossed the computer onto the couch beside her.

She glanced down at the laptop. "What's this for?"

I shrugged. "Just watch a movie or something."

"So I came over to spend time with you, and you want me to watch a movie instead?"

"You obviously don't want to watch Bathurst. I'm trying to be thoughtful."

"Fine."

I rolled my eyes. "Fine" rarely meant anything good when it came to Alyssa, but she'd opened the laptop, and I wasn't going to push my luck or it would cause more issues.

Settling back in to enjoy the race—paying extra attention during the next lap to ensure I hadn't missed anything important—I leaned against the couch. A few minutes later, I heard Alyssa sniffle. For a second, I closed my eyes and wondered just how bad it would be if I just ignored her for a while. Maybe she was just watching something sad.

Releasing my breath, and opening my eyes, I gave a quick sideways glance at her. The computer screen was off—she wasn't watching anything. I frowned and gave in to the guilt.

"Lys, I'm sorry, but you know how important this race is to me."

She nodded, but sniffed again. Then a fat tear rolled down her cheek. "I just wanted to spend some time with you. I'm sorry that I don't like the same things you do."

I swiped her cheek with my thumb. "Don't cry. Please?"

"Do you want me to go?" Her lip quivered as she asked the question and I wanted to kiss away her pain.

Turning toward her, and ignoring the TV, I took her hands in mine. "You're here now. Rather than just piss each other off, can't we spend the time together doing different things?"

She frowned and then nodded. Within minutes, she was resting her head in my lap again with the laptop open watching something—I didn't really pay attention to what. All that mattered was that I had the ProV8 series on TV, my girl beside me, and I'd narrowly avoided yet another damn catastrophe in our relationship.

THE DAYS grew hotter, and November came again. The first of the month signalled the run to the end of the school year, and the lead-up to the anniversary of our first kiss. Our relationship was still as turbulent as ever though. It was easy to blame everything else— everyone else—but it was us too. Sometimes Alyssa's moods seemed to shift without warning and she'd grow sullen and impossible to talk to.

Sometimes it was me who caused the issue. Some days it was difficult to stop the vicious words that left my mouth before I'd really thought about them—or their possible implications—all the way through.

Our life kept running the same vicious cycle. We'd date for a few weeks, maybe a month, and then be off again for a while. It was fucked up. We were hurting each other more than anyone or anything else ever could. It was worth it all though, because we also healed each other in ways no one else ever could.

Between racing, Josh's football games, and my being dragged to conferences at beachside locations with Dad's work, Alyssa and I spent more weekends apart than we did together. It sucked, but it made the desire to be near each other that much stronger during the week—when we were actually together at least. Of course, having so little time alone made us more inclined to wag school to catch up.

Alyssa was standing in front of our homeroom. She was looking for me, but hadn't spotted me yet, so I crept up behind her and grabbed her hand. Startled, she turned to look at me. I pressed my finger to my lips and pulled her along behind me. I'd been away from town for the weekend, yet another boring banking conference in Noosa that Dad had dragged Mum and me to, so I really needed my fill of Alyssa time. I knew that conversations between classes just wouldn't cut it, so I'd decided to wag and didn't give her much of an option. She knew my decision as soon as I dragged her in the direction of our park. If she had a problem with my idea, she never voiced it.

As soon as we were far enough from the school, I pulled out my mobile phone and dialled the office.

"Hello, this is Curtis Dawson. I'm calling to let you know that Alyssa won't be in school today. Unfortunately she's not feeling very well."

It was easy to convince the office staff of my story; it was all about having the right amount of confidence in my voice to bullshit my way though. Once I'd hung up, Alyssa and I burst out laughing. We were free for the day, and couldn't have been happier. I couldn't speak for her, but I'd missed the fuck out of her while we were apart and longed for some time together, just the two of us. While we walked the short distance to the park, we chatted and laughed. It was just like old times.

"Who called in for you?" she asked.

"Josh. I caught up with him just before we left."

Alyssa stepped in front of me and walked backward. "Tsk, tsk, letting his little sister wag school with strange boys. He's supposed to watch out for me."

"Strange boys?" I grabbed her waist, lifted her up, and spun her around. "I'm offended."

"Sorry." She smirked and there wasn't an ounce of apology in her voice.

"I mean, I'm sixteen, I'd say I've developed into a man by now. Wouldn't you say?"

She laughed. "But I'm right about the strange?"

"Baby, do you know anyone stranger?"

She shook her head. "You know that's what attracts me."

I grinned at her before reaching forward to brush her ponytail off her throat. It was really just an excuse to touch her.

"So, what's this in aid of anyway?" She indicated our park.

"Does a boy really need a reason to wag with his girl?"

She raised her eyebrow at me.

"Fine. I just really missed you this weekend."

"So you didn't find any easy beach babes willing to give it up as soon as they looked at you?"

"Oh yeah, loads and loads, but I bored the shit out of them all by telling them about this fantastic girl I had at home."

"And what would that fantastic girl think about this?" She waved her hand between us and winked.

"Oh, she'd be insanely jealous. She's the real jealous type you know." I beamed at her and then pushed my lips against her ear. "And she's so fucking sexy when she's jealous. Her lips plump up and a delicious blush crosses her cheeks."

"Yeah?" She blushed, which made me grin. "What else is so great about this fantastic girl?"

With a trail of kisses, I skimmed my nose and mouth across her collarbone. "Well, her skin smells like coconut."

She moaned at my touch and her breath tickled my hair.

"She's ruined me though."

"How's that?" she asked as she panted with desire.

"I can't smell coconut anymore without feeling mildly aroused."

She raised one eyebrow. "Only mildly?"

I lowered my eyes to the front of my school shorts. They were pulled and stretched out of shape by my hard-on. Her gaze followed, so I palmed myself and chuckled. "Maybe just a little more than mildly."

She brushed her hand along my side, teasing her fingers along the hem of my shirt. With a moan of pleasure building at the back of my throat, I moved my mouth from her hair to her face before pressing my lips against hers. There was no urgency in my movement. We had hours to just be with each other. My lips danced across hers without a care; our breaths were steady to prolong the kiss. For the moment, we were simply enjoying the taste of each other.

One day, maybe one day soon, we'd both take the leap beyond the two bases we'd reached together so far, but neither of us was in a hurry to push us to that next level yet.

CHAPTER  SEVEN

THE END OF SILENCE

"AND THEN SHE said that Ben told her that he loves her!" Alyssa gushed. "Isn't that great?"

I pretended to not care, but my blood burned and boiled within me. That fucker, Ben, had stolen my thunder. I'd spent the better half of the week telling him how I was building up to saying the big "L" word to Alyssa. How we'd danced around it for long enough and that I knew how I felt and was ready to voice it to her. How I had planned to do it for Valentine's Day but decided against it because it just seemed far too cliché—not to mention the bad memories that day dredged up. I didn't want to fall into the trap of doing what was expected when it was expected. Instead, I wanted to surprise her with the words at a time when I meant them the most.

Instead of letting me have my moment though, he'd obviously decided to beat me to the punch. It was ridiculous, and he'd backed me into a corner. After he'd already made that leap, if I just *said* the words to Alyssa, she'd think I was only saying them in order to keep up. I didn't want our relationship to be driven by the speed of other people.

As I read through Alyssa's math homework, checking her answers and helping make corrections, I tried to think of some way of telling her how I felt without having to just come out and say the words so soon after Ben had released them into the world.

Taking a chance, I scrawled, *Declan Reede is* at the bottom of the page.

"I mean, that's a huge step for them. Don't you think?" Alyssa pushed, distracting me from my work.

Honestly, I couldn't feel too congratulatory when it was my idea that Ben had just stolen to use first. "Yeah, it's great. Whatever."

"'Yeah, it's great, whatever,'" Alyssa mimicked me. "Are you kidding me?"

I shrugged and pulled her book out of her line of sight so that she couldn't see what I wanted to write before I'd finished it.

"I just don't see what the big deal is, Lys," I said, trying to sound nonchalant, all while trying to finish what I was writing on her page. *Madly in.* "It's just a word."

My heart pounded as I wrote the letters that spelled the word. *Love.*

"*Just* a word? How can it be just a word? It's *the* word. The word that defines where you place in your partner's life."

I shrugged again as I finished the sentence, *with Alyssa Dawson,* and nudged the book back toward her. I even tapped the page with my pen. "I just don't see it that way. Surely actions speak louder than words."

My breath caught in my throat while I waited for her to look down.

"Are you freaking kidding me?"

"What?" I said.

"You don't think people need to hear that someone loves them?"

I rubbed my hands through my hair. I was losing control of the situation, and my grand gesture had failed. I needed to convince her to look down, to see the truth.

"You hear the words thrown around so much these days. Every

celebrity is in love with someone new every week. How is that special? Maybe sometimes, you just need to open your eyes and see what's right in front of you."

She frowned.

"Let's just finish our homework, hey?" I asked.

She shut her book and leaned over the top of it. "Tell me how you feel about me."

I blinked at her. If she just looked down in her fucking book, she'd know the answer.

"Don't you feel anything?"

"Don't be stupid," I snapped. She was backing me into a corner where I felt like the only right thing to say were the three little words I'd written for her, but I didn't want to say them just because she wanted me to say them. I wanted her to know I meant them with every part of me, not just the parts that didn't want to draw out her inner bitch.

"Why is it stupid?" she shouted.

"Because you know the answer already."

"Do I?" She shoved her book into her bag before swinging the backpack roughly onto her back.

"Of course you do, Lys; you know you mean everything to me."

"Then say the words."

She just didn't get it, and the more she insisted on fighting instead of just listening to me, the less inclined I was to say anything to her at all. "I'm not going to say *that* just because someone else has or because you want me to. I don't need to compare *us* with anyone else. Why don't we get back to our homework? There was a question there I still wanted you to double check."

"So what I'm hearing is that you really don't give a shit."

"Fuck, Lys, seriously?" How could I claim any sort of feelings that were coerced out of me by anger? "I'm not going to be pressured into this shit!"

"Fine," she retorted. "No pressure. Don't worry about it."

"Good. I won't."

She grunted in frustration. "God, you're infuriating

sometimes."

"Well, you're confusing as fuck."

Slumping back down into her chair, with her backpack still on, a barrage of tears started to fall. Sometimes I really wondered what went through her head. How could she go from flashing anger to waterworks in a matter of seconds?

Part of me wanted to comfort her, part of me wanted to throw my hands in the air and say fuck it all, but all of me wanted her to stop crying.

"Just stop crying will you?"

She cast me a withering glare harsh enough to send my balls retreating into my body.

"I'm not going to say the words just because you're crying."

"Christ, Declan, you think I'm crying just to get you to say that you love me?"

"Well, I don't see any other reason for you to be in tears."

"How about having an arse for a boyfriend?" She sniffed and sobbed as she said the words.

"Well that's simple. If I'm such an arse, don't be my girlfriend."

Her tears started afresh. "Fine."

Her voice held a finality I'd heard a few times before. Each time it preceded terrible events. It was enough to stop my heart and still my tongue.

She glanced up at me from between her wet lashes, as if expectantly waiting for me to say something, or move toward her, but I felt like I was two steps behind the conversation and desperately lost.

"It's fine," she said after a beat. Her voice held a dangerous calm. "You're right. I shouldn't settle for an arse as a boyfriend."

She stood again, shoving the table at me and blocking me in. Shaking her head, she walked away. "It's over, Declan."

"What?" I couldn't comprehend how quickly it'd disintegrated from a discussion about saying I love you to her walking away declaring we were over. Again. Fighting against the desk, I pushed it away and fought my way out. By the time I did, she was already at the library door. "Lys, wait!"

If she wanted the words so damn much, I was just going to give them to her.

The door slammed shut behind her.

Fuck! I raced to the door to follow her, but I couldn't shout that I loved her across the school while she was pissed at me. She'd eventually think I only said it to stop her, and then I'd never get her to trust that I meant it the first time I said it.

"Can I come over later?" I shouted after her.

She didn't even glance over her shoulder. "I won't be home and you won't be welcome. I want to be with someone who isn't afraid to tell me how he feels."

I glanced at her bag which held her homework—and my words. I didn't want to leave it with us pissed at one another though. "But, baby—"

She spun around and raised her hand. Her eyes flashed with anger and my words froze on my lips. "Don't you 'baby' me, Declan Anthony Reede. We're through."

I'd learned a while ago when to follow her and when to let her go. This was a let her go sort of moment. She needed to simmer with her anger for a while, but that didn't mean her dismissal didn't swarm around my body and churn everything up in the meantime.

Alyssa climbed into Jade's mum's car and then she disappeared. The lump in my throat grew bigger with every minute she was out of my sight.

Mum wasn't home when I got there, so I went to Alyssa's. I knew she wasn't going to be there but I found the next best thing to my own mother instead.

"Oh, Dec, I didn't expect to see you. Alyssa's not here," Ruth said as she pulled open the door.

"I know. I just needed to see someone."

"What's up?"

I didn't really know where to begin. Honestly, I didn't really feel like talking about it. I just didn't want to be at home alone. Neither did I want to see the traitor, Ben, who'd caused the issues. I sighed in frustration. "Nothing. Can I just hang here for a while?"

She gave me a smile. "Our home is your home. You know

you're always welcome."

"Thanks."

She handed me a Coke. "If you want to chat, I'm a good listener."

I scoffed. *Unlike Alyssa.*

We sat in silence while we watched TV. After a few moments, her silence drew a question from me. "When did you know it was the right time to say I love you to Alyssa's dad?"

She looked quizzically at me, but then a knowing smile graced her lips. "I just knew."

"Did you worry that you were saying it too soon?"

"Not that I mind, but where's this coming from?"

"Lys demanded I tell her that I love her today."

She chuckled. "Why doesn't that surprise me?"

"The stupid thing is I was going to say it anyway, but instead we had a fight about it."

"She's headstrong. That's one of the things you like about her, isn't it?"

Despite the fact that my chest ached and my head swirled with doubt and confusion, I smiled. "Yeah. It's also one of the things that pisses me off about her."

Ruth laughed. "That's often the way it is with these things."

"I just hate the expectation that our relationship's supposed to follow a certain path. What's wrong with doing things at our pace?"

"There's nothing wrong with it."

"Then why's she so pissed off at me for not doing things exactly when she wants me to? Why can't I say I love her when I mean it and not just use the words to make her happy?"

"Weren't you going to say it anyway?"

"Yeah, but . . ." I trailed off. My argument died on my lips at the look on her face. "I just don't want them to be meaningless."

"Why on earth would it be meaningless?"

"It's just used too much, isn't it? Every Tom, Dick, and Harry seems to use it to get what they want these days. Where's the value in it?"

"It's not the words as such that hold the value. It's what they mean to you both."

In that statement, she'd struck a huge nail on the head for me. The one thing that had held me back in the days and weeks before whenever I'd considered saying the three words to Alyssa. "What if they don't mean the same thing to Lys as they do to me?"

Ruth wrapped her arm around my shoulders and rested her cheek on my hair. "I really don't think that's something you have to worry about."

"I just don't know. Sometimes it feels like our path is too hard." My voice trembled with the tears that threatened to fall. "We spend more time apart than we do together."

Ruth ruffled her fingers through my hair. "That's high school for you."

"Is it just that though? How do I know if we're supposed to be together or not?" Tears sprung into my eyes and I leaned farther into Ruth's motherly embrace. "It just feels like all we do lately is tear each other apart."

"Sweetie, trust me when I say things get easier once you're out of school. Right now, you're stuck in a big melting pot of hormones and stress. Things seem bigger than they will in a few years. In fact, I'm sure one day you'll look back on all of this and laugh."

"Maybe."

"If you really love each other, which I suspect you do, it'll work out eventually."

"Thanks, Ruth."

"Maybe tomorrow, you can tell Alyssa what she wants to hear."

"I wrote it in her book."

"What?"

"I wrote it for her. I didn't want to tell her, because Ben had just told Jade, but I wanted her to know."

"Well, I'm sure when she finds it, she'll appreciate the gesture."

I sat with Ruth for a little while longer, thinking about everything she'd said.

When I got home, I found Dad was back from his latest three-day banking convention. He grilled me about where I'd been and when I told him about the fight I'd had with Alyssa and my conversation with Ruth, he sat me down.

"Just be sure that this is what you want."

"What do you mean?"

"You two are very intense. You don't want to be making any decisions or choices that will trap you in the long term."

"Trap?"

"Well, you want to race V8s long-term, don't you?"

"Yeah. Of course."

"Well, how do you think kids fit into that equation? A wife?"

"Fuck. I'm just telling Lys that I love her. I'm not talking about kids or marriage."

"*You* might not be thinking of those things, but you can bet your bottom dollar that they've passed through Alyssa's mind more than once."

Past conversations rolled through me. There had been times Alyssa had spoken about those exact things. At the time, I'd thought she'd meant in the abstract, but Dad's words made me wonder. Had she meant it as an actual plan for the future, the way I talked about racing V8s with her?

After the conversation with Dad, I couldn't fight the niggle of doubt that had taken hold in my mind. I went to bed wondering whether maybe Dad was right.

When I woke the next morning, the seeds of uncertainty that had taken root the night before were still there. Accompanying them were nerves unlike any I'd ever experienced before. It was likely that Alyssa would have already found my note.

What would she think? Would she appreciate the gesture or think I was a coward for not voicing the words aloud?

My hands were sweaty and I kept fidgeting as I drove Mum's car to school in an attempt to get enough hours up in my log book before it was time to take my driver's test. Mum sat in the passenger seat talking about some crap; I wasn't really listening. It wasn't like I needed her guidance when it came to the road. I'd been driving for as long as I could remember. If I could get around a racetrack cleanly, a suburban street was hardly a challenge.

By the time I got out of the car and headed for homeroom, I was a sweaty mess. It seemed likely that I had a fifty-fifty chance of being kissed or ignored. Of having my love returned or my heart stamped into the dirt. I spotted Alyssa on a bench in front of the classroom. Her smile grew exponentially when her gaze locked with mine and all of my nervous energy rushed from me on my next breath.

My own grin grew to match hers. She'd obviously found my note. She'd found it and knew how I felt. She ran toward me, and I sped to get closer to her too.

The instant she was in my arms, all of the doubt Dad had instilled in me dissipated. Everything disappeared except her.

"I'm so sorry, Dec, I'm an idiot."

I leaned over to whisper the words she needed so badly to hear, but before I could get them out, she pressed a finger to my lips.

"I know," she murmured. "I love you too."

"Don't ever doubt it." I nuzzled her hair and kissed her neck. "No matter what happens—don't ever doubt it."

She shook her head and smiled. "Never again."

CHAPTER EIGHT

THE END OF PRIVACY

WHEN I LED Alyssa into my parents' home, my mind was filled with thoughts of the events of twelve months earlier. My birthday: the day we'd got back together after our longest breakup. This birthday had been so different already. Alyssa had met me at the school gate with my present in her hands and a kiss on her lips. Instead of spending the day avoiding each other, we'd spent it ignoring everyone else.

Before we'd even finished crossing the threshold, Mum was at the door preening over Alyssa. I stifled a chuckle. Once, Alyssa had been as much of an installation in my house as I had been in hers. It had been a while since I'd last brought Alyssa home though, mostly because her parents were home less often than Mum. Even when Josh was there, he didn't care or want to know what we did, so we were usually left alone. Whenever we were at my place though, Mum practically became a helicopter. I knew it came from a place of love, but it was still annoying as fuck to have Mum looking over our shoulders when I wanted to kiss my girlfriend.

"It's so nice to see you, Alyssa," Mum said, pulling her into a hug. Despite the fact that Alyssa was tugged away from me by the move, I refused to let her hand go.

"You too, Kelly," Alyssa replied, her voice sugar and sweet despite the things she'd been whispering to me not too long before. "Your hair looks lovely."

Mum touched her new cut and smiled before turning to me. "You hide this young woman away far too much. You should bring her home more often."

I rolled my eyes, but held my tongue. There wasn't much point trying to explain that Mum's reaction was exactly the reason why I didn't bring Alyssa home very often.

"I hope you brought your appetite," Mum said to Alyssa. "I've cooked Declan's favourite, and I've catered for an army again. You know me."

As soon as Mum's back was turned, Alyssa met my gaze, and the look in her eyes bypassed every logical part of my brain and travelled straight to my dick. *Fuck me*! I fought against the urge to drag her straight to my room mid conversation.

"I'm starved," Alyssa said. It took my mind a moment to catch up to the fact that she was talking to Mum and not me. She turned away to meet Mum's gaze, and I was finally able to breathe again. "I'm really looking forward to dinner."

"Very good. It's still another hour away, so I hope you two can amuse yourselves for that long."

Alyssa grinned at me. "I'm sure we can find something to do to occupy our time."

My throat went dry as Alyssa said the words. I hoped she meant it in the way I took it, but had no way of knowing for sure. At least until she practically pushed me in the direction of my bedroom.

Before the door had even closed behind us, her lips were on mine and my hands had found their way to her back. Without wasting a second, I unclasped her bra and cupped her boobs.

She pushed me until I crashed against the side of my bed and then she climbed onto my lap and ground her hips against mine. We'd discovered this little dance just a few weeks earlier and fuck if it didn't feel fantastic. Her tongue clashed with mine as she kissed me with a rhythm that matched the sway of her hips.

Between the feel of her silky skin and hard nipples under my palms, the relentless grinding of her heat against my cock, and the way her lips caressed my mouth and jaw, I knew I wouldn't last long.

Years ago, when I'd first discovered the pleasure of my own hand, I'd never dreamed that I could feel so damn good without direct skin-to-skin contact. Although as incredible as it felt to have her on top of me, a new fantasy struck me. I thought about Alyssa's hand snaking down the front of my pants, of her gentle caress wrapped around . . .

The thought was enough to do me in. With a grunt and a moan Alyssa stifled with her mouth, I came hard. For a moment, Alyssa stared at me as I collapsed into a spent heap. Then with a frustrated look, she grabbed my hand and guided my fingers to her centre — over the thin material of her panties.

With gentle strokes, I matched the same rhythm she'd set when she was grinding her body against me. A moment later, she tipped her face up to the ceiling as her body grew ever more restless. Her hips rocked forward, urging my fingers to press harder until I could feel her dampness through her panties. I considered how easy it would be to brush aside the thin scrap of material and touch her properly. She tilted her head down and met my questioning gaze.

With a tiny nod, she gave me permission. I groaned nearly as loudly as she did when my fingers brushed across her slick flesh.

Her hands came to rest on my shoulders and fisted in my shirt. The movement brought her body closer to mine and I could feel her hot breath rushing against my ear as she panted and gave low, almost inaudible moans of pleasure.

I reached out with my free hand, drawing her face closer and forcing her lips to mine.

"Fuck," she muttered under her breath as her body grew rigid.

"Declan. Alyssa." Mum's voice came at the exact second she knocked. But she must have pushed the door handle at the same time because the door swung open. Alyssa and I sprang apart in a flash and she crossed to the other side of my room, surreptitiously crossing her arms in front of her chest to hide the fact that her bra was unclasped.

For a brief moment, which might have been comical if not for the mortification that rolled through me, Mum's gaze swivelled from left to right, between Alyssa and me. A deep red swept up her cheeks, and from the corner of my eye, I spotted the same colour rising on Alyssa's face.

"Uh, I, um, I just wanted to see if you wanted something to drink?" Mum's voice was high-pitched and filled with nerves. Both Alyssa and I shook our heads and answered with a hasty no.

I risked a glance over at Alyssa, meeting her gaze. A nervous chuckle almost burst from me. She was bright red and flustered, whether because she'd been denied her release or from embarrassment I couldn't tell—it may have been a combination of the two. Her eyes flashed with irritation and she was glaring at me as if she expected me to do something.

"Look, Mum, sorry. Can we just have a moment?" I asked when my brain finally reconnected to my mouth.

For another moment, Mum looked a little dumbfounded, but then nodded. "Yeah, uh, yeah. Of course."

After she'd left the room, the nervous laughter I'd been holding in burst from me.

"I'm glad you find it funny, you arse!" Alyssa snapped, but there was no anger in her tone. Only incredulity and embarrassment.

"I'm sorry," I said, but I couldn't stop my laughter. I stood and crossed the room to her, trying my hardest to ignore the sticky wetness in my boxers.

Pulling her into my arms, I touched my lips to hers, even though the laughter was still on my tongue.

"It's not funny," she said, giving me a gentle nudge away. Laughter fell from her mouth as she said it though, so I knew she wasn't pissed at me. At least, not for the moment.

I moved closer to her again, pinning her to the wall with my body. My laughter gave way to desire as I drew her in for another kiss. When I moved to deepen it, Alyssa pushed me away.

I trailed my fingers through her hair and brushed her cheek. "What's wrong, baby?"

"Your mum is right outside the door!"

"Nah, she'll be in the kitchen now." I trailed my lips along the column of her neck.

"But she could come back in at any moment." Alyssa's argument was breathless and weak.

My fingers brushed along the hem of her shirt, teasing her stomach and earning a shiver in response. I walked my fingers over her silky skin, trailing over her stomach and tickling her ribs. "You don't really want me to stop, do you?"

"Dec," she murmured. It wasn't a request to stop, nor was it a plea for more. She seemed torn, but I was willing to play dirty to convince her to do things my way.

"Where was I before?" I didn't add the, "we were interrupted," because I refused to offer any reminder of the incident moments earlier and risk her stopping me. I wanted to show her how much she meant to me and finish what we'd started.

My hand brushed her thigh, and my fingers skimmed the hem of her skirt. With a desperate sigh, she tilted her head back against the wall. The small sound gave me courage and I lifted my hand higher, pushing the material up out of my way.

When my fingers reached the edge of her panties, I pushed them aside and grazed her clit.

"Oh, God," Alyssa's exclamation flowed across my skin in a warm rush.

I claimed her mouth as I rubbed the pads of my fingers back and forth across her heated flesh. Her breathing sped up and her hips bucked in time with my movements.

"Can I try something?" I asked in a hushed whisper.

"Always," she murmured.

"Tell me if I do something wrong, okay?"

She nodded.

I increased the slide of my fingers against her skin, rubbing along the length of her pussy. Her hips rocked forward in time with my movement and, when they did, I slipped the tip of my finger inside her.

The gasp that issued from her was the best sound in the world. It was part surprise, part needful, and all wanton. She wrapped her hands around my neck and used the hold to support herself as I repeated the action. I used her reactions to guide my touch, increasing the things that caused her to issue throaty, needy moans, and not repeating things that made her pull away. I brushed my thumb over her clit while sliding my fingers in a rhythmic motion until she came, desperate and panting, around my fingers.

"You are so fucking beautiful when you come," I murmured to her as I held her boneless body against my chest.

"What about—"

I silenced her with a kiss. "Just enjoy the moment, will you?"

She chuckled but relaxed against me. I picked her up and carried her across to the bed, dropping her down as gently as I could.

"Can you roll over and face the wall?" I asked.

"What?"

"I just need to sort out . . . my situation." I glanced down at my crotch. "It's uncomfortable as hell and I just need some privacy for it."

"Oh. Okay." She rolled over to face the wall as I'd asked.

I yanked off my shorts and boxers, using the dirty clothes to clean myself up before balling them up and tossing them in my hamper. I reached for clean shorts and boxers. A sound from my bed made me turn my head toward Alyssa.

She was on her side, facing me, and her eyes were wide. A grin stretched across her lips.

"What the hell are you doing?" The words left me before I could stop them. I couldn't really be pissed at her. After all, when the shoe was on the other foot, I'd copped all the "accidental" eyefuls that I could.

She looked a little contrite. "I was curious."

I pulled on the boxers. "Like what you saw?"

The corners of her lips twitched. "Maybe."

With a chuckle, I pulled on my shorts. "It's a damn sight more impressive when you work your magic on me."

She laughed in response. "I don't doubt it."

I flopped onto the bed beside her and drew her to my side. For a moment, we just held each other while we lay on my bed, silent, with our gazes locked and small smiles on our faces. Her fingers entwined with mine and our breathing fell into sync.

"This is perfect," I said after she brushed her hands through my hair.

"So perfect," she agreed.

I rolled onto my stomach, wrapping my arm over her chest. "Why can't it always be like this?"

A tiny sigh escaped her lips. "I wish I knew. All I know is that when I'm with you like this, alone, it all makes sense. When other people are involved . . . it's just different."

I rested my cheek on her chest. "I know exactly what you mean. Maybe we should just run away together? Live like this every day?"

She laughed. "It'd be nice. But where would we live? What would we eat?"

"You don't have to be the sensible one all the time, Lys. Dream a little with me, please?"

"I'll try."

We spent another ten minutes talking about what we might do if we just up and left, before I was finally ready to give up my alone time with Alyssa and head out to spend time with my parents.

The instant we emerged from my room, dinner was on the table—almost as if Mum had been waiting for us but had refused to come in to draw us out. Dad had obviously arrived at some point, and was sitting at the head of the table staring pointedly at me. I could almost hear the words running through his head—all to do with being "safe" if we were getting serious, and not getting too attached.

I held Alyssa's chair for her, earning a glare from Dad, and then Mum placed plates down in front of each of us.

"It looks lovely, Kelly," Alyssa said, as polite as always.

Mum seemed almost startled at the words—as if she'd been lost in her own world. "Oh, thank you. It's Declan's favourite."

"So what have you two been doing while squirrelled away in Declan's room?" Dad asked.

Mum kicked him under the table and Alyssa flushed bright red. I reached for her hand and brushed my thumb across her knuckles to reassure her. She glanced down at my fingers—the same ones that had carried her to pleasure not half an hour earlier—and her blush grew.

"Playing snap and doing our homework," I said, glaring at Dad and daring him to continue.

"How're your parents, Alyssa?" Mum asked, even though she'd probably spoken to Ruth no more than a week earlier.

"Good," Alyssa squeaked.

I started dinner, hoping that everyone else would follow suit and the awkward air surrounding us would die down. Unfortunately, no one else seemed ready to touch the food.

"An interesting report was circulated today at work," Dad said. I was relieved that he was changing the subject. At least, until he looked straight at me. "Did you know new estimates place the cost of raising a child in today's environment to be somewhere in the vicinity of a million dollars?"

With a groan, I rested my head in my hands. Alyssa cast me a questioning look, but I just shook my head.

"Interesting, isn't it?" Dad said. "It definitely gives you pause to consider the benefits of waiting as long as possible to have children."

"I disagree, Mr. Reede." Alyssa's voice was clear and without any waver. "A child needs love and not money. You can raise one on a fraction of that cost if you need to."

"But at what sacrifices? The child will miss out on so many opportunities."

"Opportunities that can be forged in other ways. Throwing money at a problem isn't the only way to solve it."

"How's school?" Mum asked both Alyssa and me.

I shrugged. "Okay, I guess."

Alyssa went into detail about her latest English assignment—an in-depth study of Romeo and Juliet. She made a backhanded remark about fathers putting their own desires and dreams before their child's needs, which made Dad roll his eyes. There didn't seem to be any safe topics any longer.

It was easy to see the conversation was disintegrating into something uncomfortable for everyone. With nothing more than a meaningful glare across the table, Mum and I had communicated our need to divide and conquer.

I launched into a conversation about some of the changes Dean wanted to make to the VK. Dad's eyes lit up at the shop talk while Mum distracted Alyssa just as beautifully. After the deed was done, Mum and I shared another loaded glare and a knowing nod. At least I'd avoided birthday heartbreak—for the moment.

After dinner, Dad headed for his computer and Mum, Alyssa, and I played cards for a while before Mum offered to drive Alyssa home. Of course, I had to accompany them because there was no way I was going to leave Alyssa alone with Mum, just in case the opportunity to ask about our secretive activities in the bedroom came up.

I walked Alyssa to her door and we shared one last, almost chaste, kiss on the doorstep.

"What you said earlier, about running away? You're right. Maybe one day, we should elope and just get away from all of this."

My face fell as she shut the door. She'd taken my impulsive statement about freedom and turned it into some type of marriage proposal. I wasn't ready for that. Not at all.

Maybe Dad had been right about Alyssa's dreams.

CHAPTER NINE

THE END OF WISHING

THE TRACK WAS the one place Alyssa refused to spend time with me. Even though I was going well in the series, she wouldn't come and support me. It was too boring for her, apparently.

It probably wasn't far off the truth really because once I was in the zone the car was my only focus. I couldn't afford distractions, not if I wanted to continue my fuck-hot debut year running as well as it had been. She wouldn't even come to the kart track with me, which was a little more fucked up considering that was usually just for fun. Once, I'd been able to convince Josh to go with me, but after I'd handed him his ass by lapping him multiple times he refused to go ever again.

Tightening my hands around the steering wheel, I forced myself to focus on the task ahead—the car and the race—and not concerns about Alyssa's lack of support. I barely had time for three deep breaths before the flags went down.

The thrum of the engine filled my veins and I came alive with the press of the accelerator. Just like I had for the whole season, I was feeling the car. It was nothing but an extension of me. The race, the season, it was all mine for the plucking. Turning seventeen had given me a new maturity behind the wheel and I'd taken every advantage of it for the last couple of months. Even though I was up against wannabes at least twice my age, there was no one who could touch me. So far, of the six rounds we'd raced, I'd earned a podium in them all. Three of those were in first place.

The car hugged the turns, with barely any body roll as I floated through the bends. In the car, I was at home. Nothing ever made me feel as powerful and potent as I did behind the wheel. With the narrow view of my visor, I was free. I was able to dream of the day my fantasies came to life. Unlike half the wash-ups on the track, I had the potential to make it onto the professional circuit.

I just needed the right person to notice me.

That didn't mean I was sitting back and waiting for someone to chance across me. It was already October and I only had a little over a month left to plan my next step after I graduated school. In the hope of securing a contract with a team, *any* team, I'd drawn up a portfolio detailing my successes in both the karting and sports sedan series I was in and sent it to every racing team I could.

There was one I wanted to attract the attention of more than any other though: Sinclair Racing. Their Holdens were the most formidable on the V8 track, and I'd dreamed of being in one of their cars long before I'd ever jumped behind the wheel. Even when I'd started in karts, it was with dreams of a place with Sinclair running in my head. It was their logo I imagined on my race suit when I kitted up for a race.

The only drawback with Sinclair was their location. The team headquarters were in Sydney, which meant that I'd have to move if ever I was lucky enough to be granted a position.

Alyssa and I had never really discussed whether she'd be willing to move if my dreams did come true, mostly because she didn't actually believe they would. We rarely spoke about my racing at all outside of how inconvenient practices, races, and my dream was to the time she wanted to spend with me. Her every action proved to me that she saw my racing as nothing more than an expensive and time-consuming hobby. For some, that might have been the case, but not for me. There was no doubt in my mind that I would make it one day. Someday. Somehow. And even if I did fail, it wouldn't be for lack of trying.

When it came to her dream, things were different. I'd spent so many of my precious few spare weekends with her walking around university campus after university campus. She'd initially told me there were two she wanted to look at, but that had ended up being four—including one down on the Gold Coast. She was just lucky I loved her.

By the time the flag went down at the end of the race, I was a good two seconds in front of second place. The win basically stitched up my season. There was no way anyone else could take the series from me, but that didn't mean I wouldn't be at the track the next race—the weekend after the formal. Every second on the track was practice for what was to come the rest of my life.

When I pulled the car off the track, I had a wide grin on my face. Nothing could hold me down or spoil my elation over my latest win.

Just like I always did, I left the car for Dean and his crew to pack up. I'd done my part as far as the sponsors were concerned. Before I'd even rounded the car, I had my phone in my hand to text Alyssa with my results. She didn't really care about whether I came first or last, but she would still be happy for me.

"Declan," Mum called out to me, but I ignored her to finish the text to Alyssa.

My phone was my sole focus after I hit send, certain Alyssa would text me straight back.

"Dec," Mum said again. She sounded a little breathless with glee, which was odd.

Sure, I'd all but won the series, but that didn't fully explain her excitement. It wasn't like I hadn't won a race before. Or a series for that matter. Mum was always thrilled when I won, but the tone in her voice was different.

I lifted my gaze to see a man standing with Mum. Despite the fact that he was shorter even than Mum, he had a presence which made him seem at least a foot taller. Beneath his red cap, with the logo I desired so desperately, his brown hair was clearly on the verge of giving up the fight to go grey. He looked at me with a wolfish grin on his lips, as if I was some prize pig, and my heart pounded at the sight. There was only one reason he'd be looking at me that way, and that was if he'd seen my potential.

My mouth went dry at the sight of him. It was as if my dreams had manifested themselves into reality in front of me. I'd hoped and prayed for the moment, but for it to be real, and really happening, was almost more than I could handle.

"Declan, this is Danny Sinclair," Mum introduced him, completely unnecessarily. Her voice wavered as she spoke because she knew as well as I did just how big a deal it was for Danny Sinclair of Sinclair Racing to have come to this meet just to watch me. "He received your portfolio and wanted to stop in and watch you race in person. Mr Sinclair, this is my son, Declan Reede."

"Nice to meet you, Mr. Reede." He stepped forward and offered me his hand.

I didn't hesitate to take it, but I tried not to think about how much of my future might be riding on a handshake and the conversation that would follow. "You too, Mr. Sinclair, and you can call me Declan if you'd like."

"Impressive driving out there, son."

"Thank you, sir."

"Our race strategist told me about the package you sent. It was very thorough and shows a natural talent for not only racing, but also race management."

"It is my dream to drive in the ProV8 series, sir. It has been for as long as I can remember. I will do anything it takes to get the opportunity; if that means being thorough, well I'll be as thorough as needs be."

Mum nudged me, and I realised why. I wasn't giving him the full details of my dreams.

"To be honest, sir, Sinclair is the ultimate destination for me. I would take any driving position, but your team is the crème de la crème and would be my first choice if I was given a chance."

"That is what I am here to talk to you about. Our lead driver,

Dane Kent, is retiring in the next few years. As a result, we're undergoing a reshuffle in the ranks and might just have a position opening up in the production car series."

I blinked, speechless. For all the dreams I'd had of getting a chance to go into the V8s, never in my wildest dreams had I imagined the head of a team would personally come to see me. Especially not Danny Sinclair. The man was a race legend in his own right, from back in the early days of Bathurst.

He led me away from the crowd, and Mum discreetly disappeared. While the afternoon sun dipped, I chatted with the legend. Our conversation covered everything from why I'd started in racing, why I wanted to race for Sinclair, different racing techniques, my goals in the short and long term, and whether I was happy to move to Sydney. By the time we wrapped up our chat, we were laughing and joking with one another. He seemed happy with the answers I'd given, and his relaxed smile made me relax.

With a final handshake, he told me about the contract he'd be willing to offer me. Even the starting salary was more than my father made, more than I could have ever dreamed of making straight out of school. To be paid so well for doing the one thing I loved more than anything else was almost unbelievable.

"I think you would make a great addition to our team, Declan. You would of course have to submit to the standard testing: personality, driving ability, psychoanalysis. If all of that comes back satisfactory though, you will be offered a contract in due course. With your looks and charm, I think you'll be a bit of a sponsor's delight."

When I drew my hand back, I couldn't stop the quiver that ran through me. In one afternoon, my dream had apparently become a reality. I didn't want to get too far ahead of myself—there were still lots of things to consider—but the door had been opened and all I had to do was walk through. "Thank you so much for the opportunity, sir."

"SO, MY handsome winner, what spoils will you claim for your victory?"

I hadn't told Alyssa about the conversation with Danny Sinclair or his conditional offer. Mostly because there were still so many steps to go through before I would even be considered for a contract, and there was no point stressing us both out unnecessarily if it didn't work out.

Instead, I thought we'd enjoy our last weeks of school together. In a little over a month, we'd be having our formal and graduating high school. We'd work out what came next once we got there.

In the meantime, it was still vitally important to keep my nose clean and get good grades. One thing Sinclair had specified was decent results on my high school certificate. Not because I necessarily needed the math or English skills for the job, but because it showed dedication and commitment. In each conversation I'd had with their recruitment team, those words cropped up over and over, together with the word family. Apparently, Danny didn't like to think of the team as anything less than a family.

It was why I tried so hard to concentrate on my algebra homework despite Alyssa's desire to celebrate my win. She made it harder to focus on my work by looking so damn fine as she sat on her bed, her back against the headboard and long, slender legs extended in front of her. Each time I glanced at her, I kept thinking I would much rather study *her* bra.

"Well?" She looked at me with come-fuck-me eyes.

Even after almost two years, I wondered if she knew exactly what that look did to me. I was instantly hard and all thoughts of algebra, Sinclair Racing, and everything outside of her bedroom went out the window.

I climbed onto her bed and crawled over to her. With a teasing smile, she leaned back away from me as I moved to kiss her. Our dance—her retreating while I advanced—only stopped when she was lying beneath me. Releasing a contented sigh, I captured her mouth with mine. My legs straddled her thighs, my weight pinning her gently beneath me as I kissed her with every ounce of passion I felt for her.

After we were both breathless, I moved my mouth from hers and trailed small kisses along her neck, finishing at her collarbone. With teasing nips of my teeth, I sucked her skin into my mouth, marking her as mine with a purplish blemish. As I did, she ran her hands up along my chest, undoing the buttons of my school shirt one by one.

I knew Josh, Ruth, or Curtis could come barging in at any moment. Alyssa had a lock on her door, and always kept it locked when we were alone together, but all of her family knew the secret trick to opening it with a butter knife.

After all, they'd each had to break into her room at one time or another after she'd accidentally locked herself out one way or the other. The thought that someone might come crashing through the door at any second only upped the excitement factor for me. I ran my hands up her back and she arched to make room. I undid her bra in an instant and circled my hands around to cup her breasts. She moaned as my fingertips found her nipples and traced gentle patterns over them. I continued to trail kisses up and down her neck and onto her mouth. Despite the risk of intrusion, we were in no hurry.

We'd been taking things a little further each time we'd been together. After the make-out session where we'd moved beyond dry humping to actually touching each other, things had continued to progress. We'd laid hands on, and in, very private areas and each time it had felt fucking fantastic.

She pushed me gently to roll me over so that I was the one on the bottom.

"Sit," she said, and I didn't hesitate to follow her instruction, leaning against her headboard. She sat back on my outstretched legs, gazing up at me. Her natural shyness battled with some desire brewing inside of her. The sight just about did me in. She leaned toward me again, but rather than kissing me, her lips brushed across my earlobe.

"I want to try something," she whispered.

"Anything," I managed to whisper back, despite being utterly breathless. My stomach tightened and my cock was rock hard. She had me straining for release already, and she hadn't even touched me yet. The anticipation of her touch was driving me insane, which was clearly having an effect on her too. Her pupils were dilated, and her heart beat rapidly against her ribs. I could feel it pulsing against my palm as I caressed her breasts—it was a heady sensation.

Her hands trailed down my chest, over my stomach, and onto my shorts. She fumbled with the button, obviously nervous about whatever she wanted to try. She managed to pull down the zipper and then she tugged my shorts and boxers down a little, allowing her access to my cock. It was the most she'd do to undress me. Because of the easily unlocked door situation, we'd learned not to throw our clothes off entirely. It was impossible to know when someone might come in and we'd have to scramble to dress. It was far easier to just pull up a zip than to hunt down a pair of shorts.

Her hand closed around me and my eyes drifted shut. I didn't understand why she'd asked permission to do that; it had been exactly what she'd done last time, and God, I wanted it. After a moment, I felt a shift in her position. The feel of her touch was heaven, but I needed to know what she was doing. I opened my eyes just in time to see her tongue come out and lick the tip of my dick.

Fuck me.

She caught my eye and smiled as she did it again, eliciting a moan from my lips. It was clearly what she'd wanted because she brought her whole mouth down around my length as soon as the sound had left my mouth. The sight and feel of her mouth around me, the sensation of her lips dragging down to my base, made me come on the spot. I clutched at the sheet as I exploded into her mouth. I expected her to be repulsed by the action, to jump up and make a run for the bathroom to spit it into the sink but instead she swallowed, then dragged her lips up to my tip again and released me with a smile.

"Fuck me, Alyssa."

"Soon."

"What do you mean?"

"Well, I kind of thought . . ."

"What?"

"Forget it. It's lame."

"I'm sure it's not lame." I pulled her closer to my chest, holding her in order to give her the courage to tell me what she'd meant.

"I just thought, rather than going to one of the after-parties, we could organize our own."

"Why would we do that? There's so much to organize and who'd come anyway with Blake and Darcy hosting theirs at her Dad's apartment?"

Alyssa chuckled. "No, I don't mean like that. I mean a private party. Just the two of us."

My brain caught up with my cock. "Oh! Wait, are you sure?"

"Well, it's only a month before the second anniversary of our first kiss. And two weeks before my birthday. Plus, it's the biggest night of our lives so far."

"That it is."

"Wouldn't it be nice to celebrate that *together*? Without the risk of interruptions?"

"It would definitely be special," I said.

"And memorable."

"Only if you're sure though? It's not something you can take back."

"Dec, you've had most of my other firsts. There is no one I would rather share my first time with." She brushed her hands through my hair. "I love you. You own my heart and soul, why not my body too?"

"Fuck, when you put it that way, Lys, how can I possibly refuse?"

She grinned. "You can't. That's what I was counting on."

CHAPTER TEN

THE END OF INNOCENCE

THE NIGHT OF our high school formal finally rolled around.

Even before our pact and plan to share ourselves on the night, we'd spent ages planning for the perfect evening. After we'd both agreed to give our virginity to each other as a combined graduation/anniversary present, there were a few other things to organise, but they were easy final touches for me. When the day finally came, we were both ready for it—both to say goodbye to school with the dance and to take the next step in our relationship. In fact, during the two weeks before the formal, we'd had to stop ourselves a number of times before we took things too far.

I'd arranged for my dad to hire a hotel room at the Suncrest Hotel—where the formal was being held—ostensibly to "get ready in" but I knew I hadn't fooled him and he knew the real reason. Thankfully, he kept it secret from both our mums.

For the better part of the afternoon, I was at the hotel setting up candles and rose petals around the room. I'd sourced a playlist of classical music and loaded it on my iPod for some atmosphere and set up another containing all of our special songs. I'd planned everything perfectly, and was sure nothing could go wrong. I'd even arranged for a bag of Alyssa's clothes to be collected and left in our room so that she'd be able to get out of her formal dress and into something comfortable afterward.

After dressing in my tuxedo, I went to meet my best friend, Ben, in the lobby. We greeted each other with shoulder slaps before heading to the basement for my car so we could go get the girls back in Browns Plains.

Alyssa was at her house getting ready with Jade. When we arrived, I beeped the horn as we climbed out. Alyssa and Jade came out of the house together with huge smiles on their faces. I was floored when I saw the dress Alyssa was wearing. Sex on legs was too feeble a term to describe how utterly fantastic she looked.

Her dress was a bright electric blue, floor length and *very* low cut. In fact, it may as well not have had a top; the only thing giving her any semblance of modesty were the two flimsy pieces of material which rose in triangles from her hips and climbed over her breasts before meeting in the middle at the back of her neck. Everything else above her hips was on show, including her stomach, which had an opal belly-button ring residing in the middle. Her hair was swept up into a high bun full of curls with a few loose tendrils framing her face and neck. Her make-up was light and natural, but served to enhance her features perfectly.

As soon as I saw her, I wanted to put her high on a pedestal with a plaque that read, *Property of Declan Reede*, and that thought scared the shit out of me. After all, my contract for Sinclair Racing was already well into discussions. I'd already been told I'd passed the tests. It was really just a matter of the final terms of the contract.

After I'd finally nutted up and told Alyssa about it, she kept trying to be the voice of reason—telling me I should go to uni first and get back into racing after I finished, because that way I would have a fallback plan.

In my mind, I could already see where the uni path would lead. I would go to uni for three years. In that time, I would be so busy studying that I wouldn't be able to race at all. Then when I graduated, I'd be rusty and not able to drive anyway. I'd have to settle for some lame-arse job that I would never enjoy. In that direction, my life was safe, boring. Signing off on a uni placement was akin to signing the death warrant on my dreams and that *really* scared the shit out of me. These thoughts flooded my mind almost the instant the pedestal ones left, and I wanted to run. Fast.

Alyssa smiled and wrapped herself around me and then nothing else mattered. All of that other stuff: race or uni, life in general, it all seemed so unimportant in the wake of us. Those details would sort themselves out later. Being with Alyssa, then and there, that was what was important. I smiled back at her and led her to my car.

Ben and Jade were already waiting alongside it. Ruth came rushing out of the house with a camera and we spent five minutes getting photos of us as a couple, us with Jade and Ben, just Ben and me, just Alyssa and Jade. Ruth would have kept going, except we finally escaped into the car and were away.

The dance itself went off without a hitch. We mingled with all of our friends. We headed to the dance floor for a bit of bump and grind—much to our teachers' displeasure. We said teary goodbyes at the end of the night—even though we would all be back at school the following Monday for our final week.

Eventually, everyone dispersed, mostly to go to whatever after-formal party they had arranged to attend. As they filtered out, Alyssa and I waited anxiously by the elevator, casting nervous glances at each other. The hotel room key card burned a hole in my tuxedo pocket the whole time. We were both ready, but both nervous as hell.

When we finally stepped out of the elevator onto our floor I told Alyssa to wait there. I ran into the room, turned off all the lights and lit the candles. I noticed a bottle of champagne in a cooler in the middle of the room and a box of chocolates to the side of it. I put the key card down to read the note that sat on top of the chocolates. It simply read, *Be safe*, in my father's handwriting. Underneath the paper was a strip of condoms.

After gulping down a breath, I threw the note in the bin and pocketed the rubbers. Alyssa would freak if she thought my dad knew what we were planning. Then I thought of Alyssa in *that dress* and I raced from the room to get her. I put my hands over her eyes as I led her down the hallway. I reached for the door handle to let us back in. Only the door was locked, and the key card was inside — right next to the chocolates and the burning candles.

Alyssa laughed and kissed my cheek when I told her what I'd done. Then she waited patiently next to the door as I ran down to the front desk to try to get someone to open the room for me. Once they did and we were in the room, we were both lectured about the danger of unattended candles. After the hotel clerk finally left, I sat on the couch looking sheepishly at Alyssa. I felt like I'd fucked up the whole night and that she must think I was such a loser.

Instead of laughing or calling me a fuckhead, Alyssa moved closer and ran her hand down the inside of my thigh, causing my stomach to tighten. Her soft lips brushed my cheek. With my body burning from the inside out at her touch, I turned my head and captured her mouth. I ran my fingers up into her hair, underneath her bun as I had done on so many other occasions, but my hand caught on something. Yanking at my fingers to shake them loose, I accidentally jerked her head back. I tried again to pull my hand back from her hair, but it was stuck. When I gave it a third tug, Alyssa groaned with pain.

"Just give me a second," I said anxiously, gently coaxing her to look away.

She chuckled as I started to pull out all sorts of wire and crap from her hair until I released my hand. I seriously wondered how she could have that much metal in her head and still be upright.

"Sorry, I think the hairdresser might have gone a little overboard," she said, followed by another throaty chuckle.

Ten minutes later, I finally had her hair loose and we were laughing together at the pile of fasteners.

"Are there any other traps I should know about?" I asked.

"Well, there is the chastity belt."

"There'd better not be," I murmured, sliding my hand up the outside of her thigh, pushing her dress up as I went. Once I reached her hips, I found her panties. I grazed my finger from her hip into her centre and back out. She pushed her body against my hand.

"That's lucky," I whispered.

"Maybe you need to check again?" she asked, her eyes hooded with lust.

I grinned at her. Fuck, she was a goddess. "Soon."

Full of desire, I tried my seduction again, pressing my mouth to hers. Our tongues danced together and she let me guide her against the seat of the couch. My body pinned hers and I had no doubt she could feel the hold she had over me. My cock strained for her touch, and I could barely imagine being inside her. After running my hand over her shoulders, I tried to brush my fingers through her hair again, but it was still full of hairspray. It crinkled to touch, and the sensation was distracting. I liked Alyssa *au natural*.

"Why don't we have a shower?" I suggested.

It was her turn to grin at me, her breathing nervous again. It wasn't like we hadn't seen each other naked before—but we both knew this time would be different. There were expectations and a new weight in every movement. "Okay."

I stood and offered her my hand. When she was standing, I swept my arm underneath her body, lifting her as she giggled and squealed.

"Put me down, Dec," she said through fits of laughter.

"I've got you," I said.

Her fighting slowed.

I met her gaze. "I've got you, Lys. I always will."

Her laughter and mock-fighting stopped as she wrapped her arms around my neck. She pressed her face against my chest and I could have been wrong, but I swore she inhaled.

Although she wasn't heavy, she was balanced a little oddly and her dress trailed between her legs. I kicked it out of the way twice, but the third time it tangled around my ankle. I knew putting Alyssa down would spoil the moment, so I was determined to keep going. With one leg tangled, I half walked, half hopped toward the bedroom.

I hit a clump of the rose petals I'd scattered earlier, and felt my footing slip. "Shit!"

Alyssa wiggled in my arms, no doubt sensing I was about to fall. "Dec!"

I managed to keep us both upright long enough to throw Alyssa onto the bed, but the action made the material caught around my leg pull taut and I tripped over it. The sound of ripping satin filled the air and a large section of Alyssa's skirt came away. She lay on the bed laughing as I stood, the blue material of her dress draped around my shoulders and over my head. I started laughing too and offered her my hand for the second time.

Once she was standing, I saw that what little of her dress remained intact had no structural integrity. I brushed it away with my hand and it fell to the floor. All thoughts of showers, romance and everything else flew out the window. I attacked her with the ferocity of my kiss—that's the only word for it. My mouth was urgent against hers and her tongue responded in kind. She pushed my jacket off, and yanked on the bowtie that was resting around my neck. It was like she couldn't undress me fast enough, couldn't kiss me hard enough, and couldn't touch me as much as she needed. Each item of clothing she removed was tossed across the room haphazardly. Once she'd relieved me of my shirt, her mouth moved to caress my chest, and her tongue performed minor miracles on the skin there.

I stood and unzipped my pants. I pulled them free and did a move that in the moment I thought would be impressive—I whirled them around my head before launching them across the room, straight into a fucking lamp, which crashed to the ground with a bang.

Alyssa and I roared with laughter. I had no idea how much that would cost my dad—or how many times I would have to mow the lawn to pay it off—but at that moment, I didn't care. I was right in front of Alyssa and there was nothing between us but her panties and my boxers. We met each other's gazes and she smiled before nodding.

We each made short work of our own barriers and then the reality hit me. Holy shit. We were actually going to do this. My heart hammered at a thousand RPM as I slid the condom on. I wondered whether Alyssa's heartbeat matched mine, racing in her chest and filling her with need. I leaned over her, going back to taking it slow. With two fingers on the hand cupping my erection, I teased her open. I pressed my mouth to hers and her tongue brushed against my lips.

I hovered over her with my erection straining near her entrance. She tilted her hips up slightly, pushing my fingers deeper and rubbing her wetness along the tip of my cock. I almost exploded then and there.

If we hadn't spent so many months experimenting with hands and mouths, I probably would have. I drew her into a kiss, hopeful I could distract her as I pushed into her. My biggest fear wasn't disappointing her, but causing her pain. My heart beat like a military tattoo against my ribcage, but not only out of need. I was so anxious that I might hurt her if I pushed too hard or too fast that I almost couldn't enjoy myself. As desperate as I was to claim her, there wasn't a single part of me that wanted my pleasure at any cost to her.

With a tilt of her hips, I slipped in deeper and she grunted.

"Did you want me to stop?" I asked, concerned.

She winced, but shook her head. "Just give it a second."

I stayed as still as I could, kissing her neck and face as a way to distract her. After a moment, she bucked her hips up toward me. I let her control the rhythm and the depth, but fuck it felt so good to be inside her.

After another few minutes of slow, deliberate movements, Alyssa arched her back and moaned. There was no pain in the sound, and I took it as a sign to push a little deeper. Drawing myself almost the whole way out before plunging back down again felt better than I could have ever believed, and her accompanying moan told me it worked for her too.

Staring into her eyes, I repeated the action. We moaned in unison at the sensation. Alyssa's hand found my arse and she pulled me even farther into her, hitching one leg around my waist.

"Ow, fuck," she cried out.

I stilled immediately.

A reassuring smile graced her lips. "It's all right . . . just a shock."

"Are you sure? We can try again later if you prefer."

She shook her head. "I want this. I want you."

I put my hand on her cheek and pressed my mouth to hers again, moving slowly with her. Slowly, our intensity built and my orgasm crashed over me without warning.

Shit.

It wasn't what I'd planned. I felt like a loser as I rested over the top of her trying to catch my breath. Alyssa kissed my bowed head.

"I'm sorry," I whispered, knowing she had to be disappointed.

She laughed. "It's all right."

I climbed off her, feeling myself slide from her, depleted and flaccid. She pushed herself up and rested on her elbows. After I ascertained that I was actually able to stand, I pulled the used condom off, tied it off, wrapped it in a tissue, and threw it into the bathroom bin.

Then I moved back over to the bed and leaned over Alyssa. It wasn't fair if only one of us was satisfied our first time, and I intended to rectify the issue.

I kissed her mouth deeply before trailing my lips and tongue over her chest, taking each of her nipples into my mouth in turn. My hand traced a path along her thigh, over her stomach, and then over the patch of hair at the apex of her thighs. With a gentle touch, I slipped two fingers into her, moving them slowly and steadily, rocking into her body with a rhythm I knew worked for her. She bucked against my hand and the most wondrous sounds left her lips.

She was so wet and warm around my fingers that I grew hard again in no time. Without thought, I pulled my fingers out and slid my renewed erection inside her. It felt even better with nothing between us. Pressing myself as deeply as I could inside her, I was determined to give her the same pleasure I'd just experienced. I stilled my body so that I didn't get too excited and come inside her, before rubbing my fingers and thumb along her thighs and tracing across her clit.

She moaned deeply and squeezed her legs tightly around me, pulling my hips flush against hers. My thumb brushed her clit a few more times as my lips worshipped her skin until she came hard around me. Her walls squeezed tightly around my length and my eyes rolled back as I issued a matching groan. I didn't think anything could ever feel as fantastic as what we'd just shared.

I pulled back out before I got too excited and came again. I stood and noticed a small amount blood on the sheets and around her thighs.

"How about that shower?" I asked her with a smile on my face that I thought would never leave. She reached up and I pulled her off the bed. She limped a little as she stepped away from the bed.

"Fuck. Did I hurt you, Alyssa?" I asked. The thought that I might have caused her pain twisted in my stomach in a torrent of guilt.

She shook her head. "No, it just feels . . . weird."

I wrapped my arms around her waist and kissed her neck. "We'll try again soon."

"I should hope so. I plan on doing that a lot."

"So you're really not hurt?"

She kissed my cheek in response. "I'm really, really not," she whispered into my ear as she brushed her hand through my hair.

WE SHOWERED and cleaned ourselves up. At her request, I shampooed her hair and massaged her scalp to remove all the gunk the hairdressers had used. I had to use the small bottles the hotel provided as I hadn't thought to bring anything special with me. It was nice knowing that she'd be back to the natural Alyssa I loved again—free of hairspray and make-up—once we were out of the shower.

While she finished in the bathroom, I headed out to get dressed and frowned when I once again saw the slick of blood across the sheet.

Fuck, I must have hurt her!

I closed my eyes and sighed, hating that I'd done anything to cause her pain. Slowly, sense started to return to me. If it hadn't been me, it would have been someone else. Someone who might not have had any regard for her well-being at all—who would have taken his pleasure and not given a shit about her needs. Even if I had hurt her, I'd given her pleasure too.

Knowing she would be embarrassed by the sight of the blood, I remade the bed to hide the small stain. When she came back out wearing one of my t-shirts and a pair of baggy boxers, we curled up underneath the blankets with matching contented smiles on our faces.

Lying together, talk turned to other things. Her fingers played with mine as we both stared at the ceiling. Neither of us seemed willing to touch on the one topic that was certain to cause an argument—my potential race contract that she seemed convinced would never come.

"How many kids do you think you'll have?" she asked dreamily as she started to succumb to sleep.

"Fuck, Lys, please don't talk about kids after we, you know."

She chuckled. "After we what, Dec? Had sex?" She rolled over and rested her head on my chest. "It's just a question."

It wasn't *just a question* though. Not for me. It was loaded with consequences and choices. How could I even think about kids until I had my career set up? Even then, there were risks in the job. Could I subject children to that? Then there was the simple fact that I just didn't know if I wanted kids—ever. "I don't know what to say. I don't really want kids."

"What? Ever?"

"Maybe one day. A long way away. After I've done what I want to on the track."

She frowned at the mention of racing, before rolling onto her back. "I think I'd like two. A boy and a girl, just like Josh and me."

With her words rolling in my mind, I tried to turn the conversation away from the unsafe topic of the future. Instead, we chatted about what we had planned for the last week of school and then our plans for Schoolies week.

As we talked, she eventually succumbed to sleep. I was too mesmerised by her and by what we'd discovered together to relax though. Thoughts of sharing those things over and over with her in our hotel room as we celebrated the end of school with our friends at Schoolies consumed me.

While she slept, she gravitated even closer to me until she was curled under my arm with her head on my chest. Then she started to talk. At first it was nonsense, about the school exams we had just finished. About her mum. Her friends. After a while, it turned serious. "I love you, Declan."

I squeezed her a little tighter. After our argument over using the L word we used it somewhat sparingly. We'd both agreed we'd rather it mean something when we said it rather than have it become a flippant term for every greeting or parting.

"Of course, I'll marry you."

What the fuck?

My eyes shot to the smile that graced Alyssa's lips. The words rang in my head together with her earlier questions, and all of the doubts I'd ever had came flooding back. It was evidence of Dad's words. She wanted marriage. Kids. The boring suburban life that was sure to follow three years of uni.

I extricated myself from her hold and climbed out of the bed. After pacing for close to an hour with all my fears racing through my head on a never-ending loop, I spent the rest of the night sitting on the couch staring at nothing. I didn't want that life. I didn't want to be the small-town boy married out of school. I had fucking dreams and one thing was becoming clear.

From that point on, they couldn't include Alyssa "small town" Dawson.

CHAPTER ELEVEN

THE END OF THE DREAM

YAWNING AS SHE walked, Alyssa headed out from the bedroom to sit with me on the couch. My shirt hung to one side, exposing the soft curve of her shoulder. Her hair was piled like a haystack on her head. She'd smoothed it into a ponytail as best as she could without a brush, but because she'd slept with it wet, the curls were out of control.

She climbed lazily onto my lap and wrapped her arms around me before planting a kiss against my throat. I put my arms around her too and pressed my cheek against the top of her head. I didn't want to admit to the fact that I'd been up the whole night worrying about something she'd said while she slept. The smell of her had a calming effect on me. It drove thoughts of leaving from my mind. Maybe I'd just been scared. I could get past fear—I wasn't a fucking coward. I gripped her tighter, almost afraid to let her go.

"What's the matter, Dec?" she asked, pulling back to look at my face.

I shrugged. I didn't know how to voice what I felt. On the one hand, I knew she was all I ever wanted, but on the other I was terrified of being that dependent on someone. Of needing them as desperately as I needed oxygen. I couldn't imagine being tied down at just seventeen. Or giving up my dream.

"I can't believe we only have one more week left of school," she said, trying to distract me from my reverie.

I nodded.

"Have you thought some more about going to uni? I really think that's the better option in the long run."

I shrugged.

She scrunched her eyebrows together. "Declan?"

I looked into her eyes and I was her captive. The doubts I had seemed crazy. She was it for me, I knew it. Everyone knew it.

Everything else will work itself out, right?

I leaned closer and kissed her and she quickly reciprocated. When I closed my eyes, I saw the life she'd obviously been dreaming about the night before: her in a white dress walking toward me down the aisle, a house in the suburbs, kids.

Fuck!

I was too young to have kids—I was too young to even be thinking about having kids. I pulled away from the kiss and shifted Alyssa onto the couch next to me. I stood and walked to the table, leaning against it in an attempt to catch my breath.

"What is it? You're starting to scare me." Alyssa walked up behind me and wrapped her arms around my waist. Her voice was strained and tight.

I turned toward her and unwrapped myself from her arms. "I don't want kids."

"What?"

"I don't fucking want kids. I don't want to get married. I don't want any of that shit."

"What are you talking about, Dec? Where is this coming from?" She grabbed for me again, pressing herself tightly against me.

"It's what you want, isn't it? Uni. Kids. Marriage."

"Sure." Her voice was slow, cautious. "I mean, eventually."

I shook my head, trying to clear it. "I don't want any of that shit."

She didn't say anything, just tightened her hold on me. I closed my eyes and tried to use her presence to calm myself, but it just made me see that life more clearly and that scared the hell out of me.

"I want to race."

"What?"

"When the contract for Sinclair Racing comes in, I want to do it. I'm *going* to do it."

"I thought we'd discussed going to uni together and then seeing what options we had after that."

"No, Alyssa—*you* discussed that. You've never once asked what I want." I pulled away from her again and held up my finger to tell her to stay away.

She gasped. "Declan?"

"You don't think I can make a career of racing, do you?"

She looked into my eyes for a few seconds and then shook her head slightly.

"You've never even seen me fucking race."

"Well, I'm sorry that cars bore the shit out of me."

"I fucking let you drag me all around that fucking university open day, and yet you've never once come to watch me race."

"That was for both of us."

"No, that was for what *you* wanted for both of us."

"Fuck that, Declan." She was shouting at me now. "Can we not get into this shit today?"

"Why not? It's as good a fucking day as any other."

"I'm not having this same argument again and again."

"Maybe we keep having it because we're kidding ourselves that we're meant to be together."

"Maybe!" she screamed. She stalked into the bedroom and before I knew what was happening she was walking back out, carrying her bag and the remnants of her dress. She pushed the hotel room door open and stormed out. I watched after her for a few seconds, confused about what had just happened. I heard the elevator ding and everything caught up. We'd just broken up. Again.

After the best night of my life, I'd thrown it all away.

Fuck!

I ran down the hall just as the elevator doors closed in front of her tear-streaked face.

WHEN I saw Josh waiting on my doorstep, I'd thought he'd come to deliver a message from Alyssa, like he had so many times before when we'd had a break. I felt terrible about the things I'd said to her, and for the way we'd ended it that morning, so I was actually glad to see him. Hopefully it meant Alyssa and I could sort some shit out before any long-term plans were set. It had been a while since he'd last played messenger—not since he'd left high school himself—but I figured Alyssa had decided we needed an impartial third party this time.

"Hey, Josh," I said. "How's Alyssa? She was really pissed at me when she left—not that I can blame her."

His reply was a fist to my stomach with such force it made me vomit. He waited until I finished heaving, then he pulled me back to my feet by my shirt collar.

"You stay the fuck away from my sister. I would never have believed you to be capable of that fucking shit, Reede." His eyes were narrowed and full of anger.

"You're acting like it was all my fault. She's the one who fucking walked out in the middle of it!"

He roared at me as he started his attack again. His fist connected with my eye. Then his hand was in my hair and he pushed my face downward at an alarming velocity. His knee rose toward me just as quickly and impacted with a nauseating, wet thud that I felt through my entire skull. Blood trickled from my mouth and nose. I spat out a mouthful and launched at Josh in return. It didn't matter though. I may as well have punched a brick wall for all the impact I had. All I did was burst my knuckles open.

He pulled my collar again, the front this time, and held me up off the ground and close to his face. He waited until my eyes were focused on his face and then he hissed venomously, "You fuck with

Alyssa—you fuck with me. You remember that, Reede."

He pushed me back into the brick wall of the house before climbing into his car and driving away.

I slumped to the ground; the bricks bit into my shirt and ripped it as I went. I didn't care about that though. I didn't care about my face, or any of my injuries, either. Because none of that mattered, and none of it hurt nearly as much as the gaping hole that opened in my chest as I realised Josh's attack *had* been a message from Alyssa.

I knew Josh well enough to know he would never have done that on his own, not over something as stupid as an argument. After all, Alyssa and I argued all the time, but we'd always made up. His visit was obviously her way of telling me she didn't want me anymore. That if I couldn't commit to uni and marriage, and fucking kids, then she didn't want to be with me anymore.

I'd made my case pretty fucking clear on those issues that morning.

She'd just made her point equally as clear in return.

As the hole in my chest gaped wider, I couldn't get enough oxygen. Every breath I took pushed me closer to the edge. My head spun. I leaned my head forward into my lap. Tears sprang unbidden to my eyes. Then I cried. I bawled. Over Alyssa.

My tears ran freely down my cheeks, mixing with blood from my split skin before forming splotchy patterns on the concrete. I tried to breathe, but every time I did, I found that everything smelled and tasted like the blood that ran thickly down my throat. When the blood hit my already agitated stomach, I vomited. Again and again my stomach clenched and I heaved until there was nothing left.

Panic rose within me and made the tears fall faster. I couldn't breathe and my heart raced so fast and hard I was certain it would give up at any second. The bitter taste of blood still tainted my every breath. My stomach twisted against itself in its empty state.

My father came home to find me doubled over on the concrete. He raced into the house and grabbed an ice pack and a towel before leading me to the car. I pressed my forehead into the cool glass and cried the whole way to the hospital. When he asked what happened, I made up some lame story about being mugged in the city. I didn't want to answer the questions that would be raised if anyone knew Josh was responsible.

My father asked how I'd managed to drive in that condition, but I just refused to answer him. He stopped pressing for details fairly quickly, almost as if he sensed there was something I didn't want to tell him. He didn't ask how my night with Alyssa went. There was little doubt in my mind that he would have known about the broken lamp, the unopened champagne, and probably the lockout as well. I was certain he'd probably pieced everything together to come close to the truth, even if he didn't know the full details.

When I got home from the doctor's, I headed straight for my room. From wall to wall, it was stuffed with memories of Alyssa and me. In particular, there was one photo of the two of us from a school trip to Movie World. Without even thinking about it, I stalked to the photo and ripped it from the wall.

"Fuck you, Alyssa," I said through my tears as I tore the photo into pieces. "Fuck you, and your brother, and your kids and your goddamn marriage."

CHAPTER TWELVE

THE END OF IT ALL

IN THE END, I missed the last week of school because of the damage Josh had caused. That whole week, I had two black eyes, a swollen cheek, severe bruising down my left side, and ringing in my ears. Worse than any of the physical injuries, though, was the gaping chasm that had replaced my heart. No matter what I tried, it wouldn't close.

Alyssa tried to call on the first day I missed school, but I just pressed ignore each time her name popped up on the screen.

On the Tuesday, she called again. This time I spoke to her, cutting her off before she could say anything and telling her that Josh had made her point very fucking clear thank you very much, so leave me the fuck alone.

On the Wednesday, I got my contract from Sinclair Racing. Mum, Dad, and I sat around the dining table with the contract sitting in the middle. With the tension in the air, it was almost as if we were playing a game of Russian Roulette. In a way, I guess we were—just with my career.

"Are you certain this is what you want?" Mum asked. "It's a long way from home. A long way from us." *A long way from Alyssa*. I heard the words even though she didn't say them. Ever since the contract appeared and the vague possibility of me leaving home had manifested, Mum had become an advocate of caution.

There was so much I would leave behind if I signed on the dotted line. It was likely that I'd never get a second chance at success though. It wasn't like there were hundreds of openings in the field every year.

"It's everything we've been working toward," Dad said. "How can you refuse such a generous offer that will bring you all of your dreams?"

When I glanced at him, I could practically see the dollar signs rolling through his eyes like they did on cartoons.

"There's more to life than money and success. There's family. Family matters, doesn't it, Declan?" She looked to me to support her argument, but I was lost.

My mind was with Josh, reliving the beating he'd given me. It was with Alyssa as we'd kissed for the first time—and as we'd given ourselves to each other. It was mourning everything I'd lost, celebrating everything I'd gained, and spinning in relentless circles of guilt, confusion, and overwhelming betrayal. That's what Alyssa had done—she'd betrayed me by getting her brother to deliver the message so savagely.

"He's got years to worry about family and settling down. Right now, he's young and he's unattached. There's nothing holding him back." *Like Alyssa.* Again, the words never left his lips but I heard them as plainly as any he'd spoken. "Isn't this what you wanted, young man?"

I stared toward the contract again, the Sinclair Racing logo branded onto the front page, and took a deep breath. Mum and Dad continued to debate. Even though I tried to listen to them both, and consider the different options, all I could hear was Alyssa's voice. *"One day, Dec, you're going to have to choose between the damn karts and me."*

It wasn't karts though; it was ProV8s, everything I'd ever dreamed of. I'd considered my options again and again since my fight with Alyssa, and since Josh's *message*, and I wanted to sign the contract. I wanted to race. How many other options did I have, after all? It was that or go back to Alyssa, begging on my knees. Go back to the small-town plans of uni, marriage, and kids.

Ignoring Mum and Dad as they talked themselves in circles, I released my breath in one sharp exhale, picked up a pen and signed. The sound of the pen scratching across the page was enough to draw their attention.

"This is what I want," I said when Mum opened her mouth — no doubt to question me again. "It's the only thing I want."

Because I was still a minor, one of my parents had to sign the contract as well. Before Mum could even attempt to talk me out of it, Dad's signature joined mine. I nodded my thanks.

It was done.

ALYSSA CALLED again after school had finished, sobbing down the phone line and begging me to see her again so she could explain what had happened. I agreed, but only because I needed to tell her I was leaving. After my move to Sydney was scheduled, I'd become firm in my decision and I had no intention of returning home.

Ever.

That was how I ended up face to face with Alyssa on the Saturday night exactly a week after we'd given ourselves to each other.

It was the worst fucking night of my life.

The only thing I promised myself was that I wouldn't cry, and I wouldn't back down. I wouldn't leave her with the image of me as a weakling. I would be strong, and leave her with the knowledge that I was doing what was right for me. And for her too.

She sat next to me on the table. Her eyes were already red-rimmed before she'd arrived. Her hair was pulled back into a haphazard bun. She didn't look like she'd paid any attention to her clothes or appearance at all before leaving the house to see me.

"Declan," she started as her gaze assessed the heavy bruising that was still evident around my eyes and cheekbone. "About

Josh . . . I just wanted to say . . ."

"Don't," I said, cutting her off. "Just fucking don't. I don't want to know why you made him do it. I really don't fucking care. Consider your message delivered."

"What message?" she asked, sounding as confused as she had when I'd said the same thing to her over the phone.

"Fuck it. Whatever. It doesn't matter anymore." I yanked my fingers through my hair. "The only reason I agreed to meet you tonight was to tell you I'm leaving."

My voice was hard because I couldn't cry. I wouldn't allow myself to show any emotion. I couldn't or I would crack.

"What?" she asked, breathless. Her tears spilled over again. It was almost enough to make me lose it too. Almost.

I bit the inside of my mouth to stop my tears.

"I told you before. I want to fucking race." My voice quivered slightly. I stopped, cleared my throat, and continued. "The contract came. I'm going to Sydney to race. It's a done deal."

"But Declan—"

"Don't, Lys. It's signed. I'm not going to change my mind."

"So that's it?" Her anger broke through her tears. "No fucking discussion? Just an 'I'm leaving.'"

"This is for your benefit too," I murmured.

"How the fuck do you figure that you leaving is for my benefit?" she snapped.

"Because you want things that I can't fucking give you. Things you deserve. You deserve happiness, Alyssa. It just can't be with me."

Her tears were joined by chest-wracking sobs. It took everything in me not reach out to comfort her. "But it's *you* I want, Dec. I don't give a shit about anything else."

"You do, Alyssa. You might not think so, but you do."

"Don't try to tell me my own mind. I fucking know what I want. *You*."

I shook my head. "It's too late, Alyssa. I leave on Monday."

She recoiled as if I had slapped her.

"Monday?" she asked breathlessly.

I nodded.

"What about Schoolies?"

I shrugged. "Go by yourself. Or don't go at all. I don't really give a shit."

She dropped her head into her hands and a wretched sob escaped her lips. I acted instinctively, pulling her into my chest, and she cried against me.

"Don't go," she whispered, her voice strained and broken. "Please."

She pushed her face up to mine and I felt her warm lips moving against me. My own moved against her in response. My tongue worked its way into her mouth, and fuck, she tasted good. It was almost enough to break my resolve. Almost, but not quite.

I finally remembered myself enough to push her face gently away from mine.

"I'm sorry Alyssa." I bit back my own tears and ignored the chasm tearing open my chest. "This is what I want."

"And you don't want me?"

"No."

She slapped me and then stalked off into the night.

Good riddance, I thought as a way to stop the pain that held my aching heart in a vice-like grip. It was done, and Alyssa hated me; we were over for good. There would be no more on/off, just a permanent, unending off.

There was no reason for me to ever see her again.

GET READY TO START YOUR ENGINES. DECLAN REEDE: THE UNTOLD STORY CONTINUES IN

DECLINE

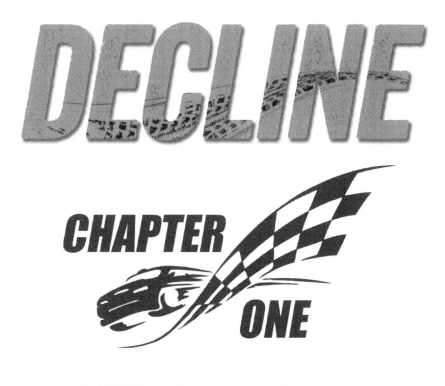

DECLINE

CHAPTER ONE

BATTLE AT THE MOUNTAIN

MY CAR THRUMMED to the tune of the V8 under the bonnet. Each time my foot grazed the accelerator, an angry growl reverberated around me. The sound coursed through my body like fuel burning through my veins and sent exhilaration rushing through me. Black bitumen stretched out as far as I could see, filling my narrow field of vision with the only sight I needed to truly feel alive. The track, and my place on it, was all I cared about.

In the distance, crowds pressed against the fences, pushing each other and vying for the best position to see the start of the race. They would watch me leap from pole position and gain further advantage over all of those lined up behind me. There was no one in front of me. No one to come between me and my victory.

No one but me—my fucked-up mind.

Realistically, I should have been buzzing with confidence, like I had been the last time I'd lined up for this race, but I wasn't. Instead, a constant loop of all the reasons I was going to fail ran through my mind, diminishing my purpose and causing my hands to shake. I tightened my grip on the wheel and took a deep breath to steady my nerves. Another press of the accelerator—another roar from my beast—reminded me of the power I wielded. The whole scenario was almost achingly familiar. My last eight starts had been from pole position, but my last five races had ended in a DNF. Did. Not. Finish.

I couldn't even get one damn car around a simple fucking racetrack in a series of clean laps. Not anymore. Not since Queensland Raceway. I couldn't explain it exactly, but every time I'd felt close to victory, something clicked out of place in my mind and for a tiny moment everything fell down around me. It shouldn't have been an issue; it was barely a lapse in concentration. It was a problem though, because it always happened when I was barrelling down a straight at speeds just shy of three hundred kilometres an hour. At that speed, even a fraction of a second was too long, especially if the straight ended with a sharp right corner.

This time, I was lined up for the fucking Bathurst 1000. A partnered endurance race. It wasn't only my arse on the line this time. My co-driver Morgan McGuire's championship hopes were resting on our joint performance. He'd already taken a moment before I'd climbed into the car to warn me of precisely what he would do to me if I managed to total the car this time. It involved a pair of rusty pliers and a part of my anatomy that I was particularly fond of.

I brushed my foot over the accelerator again, taking comfort in the snarl that issued. The car was the best it had ever been. No doubt that was partly in thanks to the complete rebuild it had needed after my last outing, but I chose to ignore that fact. I tried to focus on the roar of the engine and not on the fact that my team had informed me that I actually was close to getting one record this year.

According to Sinclair Racing's bean counters, I was one wreck away from passing the all-time repair cost in a single season. Suffice it to say this wasn't the record they, or I, wanted. In fact, Danny Sinclair and his board were so unhappy with me at the moment that it was highly possible one more wreck would see me lose not only the championship—which was all but out the window anyway—but also my career. And I fucking loved my job. I was living my dream.

It wasn't just the fast cars and loose women that excited me, although they were a benefit. A distinct benefit. My mind wandered to replay the previous night's activities with a pair of girls. There was nothing they hadn't let me do to them. By the end of the night, I'd screwed both of them in every way possible before sending them on their way.

Swallowing heavily, I discovered that thinking about my night-time activities at that moment was not the best idea. I needed the blood to stay where it belonged—in my head—and not be rushing south to fill my cock. I shifted in my seat and focused on the track in front of me and the chatter of my team in my ear.

In mere minutes, I would have to wrestle a six-hundred-horsepower, thirteen-hundred-kilogram roaring beast around a racetrack. That couldn't be done with a distracted mind. Especially not at Bathurst, a track that required the utmost concentration from even the best of drivers. Like I used to be. Before Queensland.

I closed my eyes, blocking out the track in front of me as the thought struck. Just twelve short months ago, I'd been at the top of my game. King Shit. No one was able to touch me when I was on the track. I had started the previous season as the dark horse, one that couldn't possibly be a threat, but I'd finished as the youngest driver ever to win the championship. At my age it was a fucking miracle I was in the car at all, let alone being discussed as a possibility for lead driver within the next few years. Or at least I *was* being discussed. Now, after a string of incidents, I was practically a wash-up who couldn't even finish a race. I was barely twenty-two, and my career was already hitting the skids. Unless I pulled a miracle—and a finish—out of my arse, I was finished. The chequered flag would drop on my career and I'd never see the track again. At least, not for Sinclair.

The drivers behind me revved their engines in anticipation of the start, reminding me of where my attention should have been. My mind raced with too many thoughts, and I tried to push them out, to focus only on the most important of them all. Number one: I needed to get away clean. Number two: I needed to keep my head on the track. At least that way I might have a fighting chance of finishing, which would be fan-fucking-tastic.

I can do it. The thoughts I'd been trying to keep at bay, to keep off the track, started to flash in my mind. I beat back the vision, refusing to let her screw with my head before I'd even started.

Can't I?

My head spun as the doubt crept in. I pushed it down and decided that maybe that's all I needed to do: think positive or some shit. Be the change I wanted to see in the world and all that other bullshit.

Or maybe I should just try to stop over-fucking-analysing everything.

The simple truth was that I needed to spend more time focusing on the race and less time chasing the doubt that raced through the memories in my own fucking head. If I worked out how to do that, I might stand some chance of salvaging something of the shit that was left of my life. I just couldn't see a way past my particular issue. At least none that I wanted to do.

A voice in my ear confirmed the flags were due to go up in less than a minute. I allowed myself one second of solitude and closed my eyes. Pressing my foot deep onto the floor, I listened to the throaty roar that issued from my beast. It blocked out all other sounds and left me with a moment of peace.

My eyes snapped open as I heard the familiar sounds signalling me that it was time to go. The instant the green flag was raised, I jumped. Wrestling the heavy car into line was never an easy task—stalling was always a concern—but I got away clean.

Ride on instinct.

Don't think.

Don't overthink.

You know what you need to do.

Just. Fucking. Do. It.

ABOUT THE AUTHOR

Michelle Irwin has been many things in her life: a hobbit taking a precious item to a fiery mountain; a young child stepping through the back of a wardrobe into another land; the last human stranded not-quite-alone in space three million years in the future; a young girl willing to fight for the love of a vampire; and a time-travelling madman in a box. She achieved all of these feats and many more through her voracious reading habit. Eventually, so much reading had to have an effect and the cast of characters inside her mind took over and spilled out onto the page.

Michelle lives in sunny Queensland in the land down under with her surprisingly patient husband and ever-intriguing daughter, carving out precious moments of writing and reading time around her accounts-based day job. A lover of love and overcoming the odds, she primarily writes paranormal and fantasy romance.

Comments, questions, and suggestions for improvements are always welcome. You can reach me at writeonshell@outlook.com or through my website www.michelle-irwin.com. Thanks in advance for your correspondence.

You can also connect with me online via
Facebook * Twitter

If you enjoyed this book, please let others know by sharing your thoughts on the *Decide* page on Goodreads, Booklikes, Amazon, and your other favorite review sites.

If you want regular updates, join the mailing list at www.michelle-irwin.com

Thank you

20236143R00078

Printed in Great Britain
by Amazon